MY

DOVER DAYS

By

Anju Prasad

Published by Poetry Planet Publishing
Designed by Tess Ritumalta
Edited by Marie Ezekiel

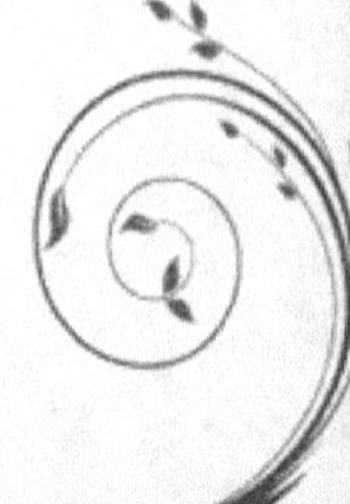

INTRODUCTION

Anju Prasad as I know her, as a poet has written a bulk of poetry. She is alive, present in several social media international poetry groups. She made efforts to let her voice be heard and many times, I felt that she wanted to be the voice of the unheard. She used to say she began her literary life, quite early scrapped poems in her childhood. She emerged as a published author in 2013 by composing a poetry collection in her native language which translated as cries of the shadow less, Anju became an International Author, by publishing Love Anthems, which was selected for many international book festivals, and she had a prestigious blue ink review on her poetry collection.

Anju's poems are deep; they addressed many perspectives of life. Her own life's battles are often reflected in many of her verses. She embraced the Asian culture vehemently, at the same time in her we could also find a woman who would stand up for rights and she personifies every woman who would stay their grounds, feet tight and head held high. Her novel," Female face of God" published by Green books is just an example of her way of looking at life and her belief in the Feminine divine, that questions patriarchy at its very roots, which is reflected in most of her verses. In surviving her tempest of life as I know Anju as her publisher from the time she wrote her poetry collection in 2018" Virginia Blues ", Anju and her poems appeared to me as victors of every storm she has been through.

Unconditional love that transcends all kinds of hatred throbbed in her poems. It always captivates the soul and Anju finds her poems as a means of communication. Through her poems she believed she could inspire the wounded and broken souls and this was one of her great ambition, she always discussed during our communications. Anju's poems were like young sprouting springs in Love Anthems; she was working and living in Kuwait those days. They were bright, colorful, dreamy, and mystically beautiful whereas in 2018, In Virginia Blues, I found her initial vibes of a pink blossom paving a way into melancholic autumn melodies as she would refer them to which reflected her passion and success and total breakdown. It was her struggling days that brought us together, I write this because I wanted to say even if some lives are broken to the limits that it seems it can't be patched, Anju, her life and her poems says you can if you think you can.

This poetry collection is her rising, her transcendence in a silent and in a deep loving way. Anju's reflections, her ironies made her poems moving. She touched many hearts, with words when she stumbled with her demons. Anju's poems gleamed with love, harmony, courage, and such great insights, which she was building in her own life, I could see as a friend, poet, and co-traveler. Her emotional and professional crisis, and the social abandonment she went through, with utmost integrity never made her discouraged mirrored in her poems strongly. Her poems bloomed with fragrance of a highly spirited individual who wished to serve the community she existed selflessly, calling forth for such a movement.

Anju's poems touch every shade, she is the protagonist and the antagonist, she represents her characters and her heart transpires through them. I wish through publishing and giving life to them I am spreading a message to every single person in this world who faces catastrophes relentlessly making them unable to upsurge, there is hope in every despair and there exist such poets like Anju who tries to convey themselves to the whole world, to never give up and to trust and keep going…

Many poems in this collection are pearls extracted from the oysters of her profound thoughts, esoteric, and her knowledge of several other art forms blended with her pain and perseverance. Any reader could easily go through the plains, of the trance of her poetic excellence, unleashed with serenity and spiritual longing pining in it.

I wish her the very best in her effort to use her inherent talent to converse with the universe, the love that she has for humanity and those who are suffering at hands of insolent might. She has dedicated this book to all those people who undergo a mental health crisis who are abandoned by dear and near. For her life is a poem and it says, Behold, rise, you can ….

Lovely Garcia,
Writer and Publisher
Poetry Planet Publishing House

Table of Contents

Coza
2015

A WOUNDED LIONESS

In the deep dense forest

where justice becomes a fun

every day and injustice rule the land

in such a famous soil I live

I, a wounded lioness.

Friends, a wounded lioness

who is a mother that watches her tribe.

When such a lioness goes hunting,

It is just a poignant scene, nothing matches it

All she wants is to protect

She is such a wounded soul.

Who hunts not to get hunted by

who knows she can't even trust

her own shadow that follows

and every time it is none but

a loved one just backstabs and smile

at your face, so sweet at your fall.

This world is full of treacherous wolves

or cunning jackals, or fox, or hyenas

and vultures that wait for your carcasses.

But a lioness doesn't just fear,

she doesn't take her heart to rest in the

care of a fortress of a male's heart,

the most deceiving of it all.

So she walks in pride to take care of the "pride"

How could your world silence her?

Who has crossed boundaries

of right and wrong you defined

And defined her own for herself

And will fight your merciless acts.

I am such a lioness whose faith in herself

are so rooted that you can't break it like

molten lava which is engraved in blood and sweat of

hardships and toil of pain and pressure that none can

ever fathom.

I am still that Lioness who is alone in her path

whose language was love once and is the vengeance of

course now I defer not

Oh this land I honor you

for what you have made out of me!

A lioness wounded... mighty

who is watchful every minute

Caring and daring- no coward

A proud female of my kind.

MY CONTEMPLATION

In the deep solitude of splendidness that reverberated in
the very valleys of Indus

where originated the eternal art of seeking into the

self-nudging the creation of civilization at its behest,

there I nail my unquenchable yearning to know,

the great philosophy of my Nation vibrating in it.
In the hermitage of soil that is made souls

Where syllable sang primordial bliss of existence,

 I am gifted with words enthralling with a generation

who were enlightened burning in the flame of their own
self -actualization

 My land I honor my inheritance of everything beautiful

 that I comprehend abstract and concrete, painful

and joy and everything I take pride.
Into the pining thirsty lips of oysters of every single
matter,

 of this cosmos when the unequivocal silence broke in as
a big bang

on and flew down as ecstasy that manifested the now

When Time the supreme consciousness rejoiced in it

I ask that omnipotence a portion of its contentment as
mine

I realize the unconditional love of that universal

the mind is dormant in every atom I see.

I am astonished at the immense power of such

un imaginational love making God particles alive

My poems let them unleash and I believe when

rhythm beat and notations with movement blends
synchronizes

it evokes a giant wave-form of love that heals ...every
vice every

evil every pandemic

Let my words seep in every mind as new blossom and
sprouts of spring

when I go into deep contemplation in my thoughts.

Let the forest the farm-lands the plains,

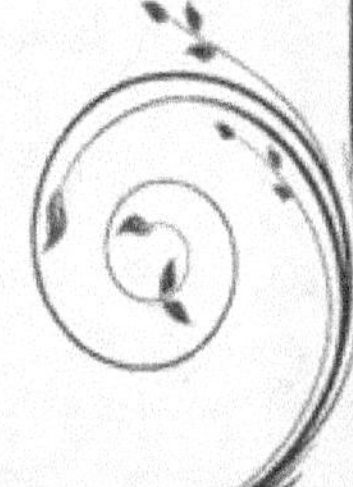

the river-beds, the hills, oceans, and moon of our milky
way,

rewrite the equations that pertain and persist in the word
deciphering it as peace and harmony.

Of all the victories and assets.

6 FEET

Of all the victories and assets

How much do we require

Just a 6 feet

Why do we fuss and mess

Of all the belongings and acquisitions

How much is going to be ours

Just a 6 feet

Why do we seek to strike and fret

Being in a religion that prepares

A pyre is just to be ashes to ashes

This whole plight of flight and fight

Where are we losing

To hail God he or she did not ask you

God is unconditional love

To debate on political satire

That world is going through

You are just an atom thinking

You matter most in the molecules of every matter.

Why break your mind on theories of relativity

Why code programs for future robotics

When a single virus can wipe off the universe

Silent mocking at your face

You are masks reduced to masks

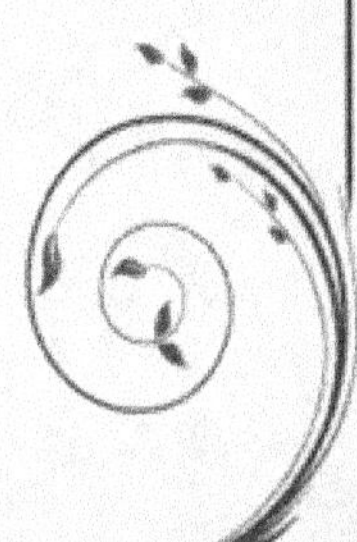

In today's world

Faces that reflect an emotionless heart

Good, it befits.

Love is an old world and lust

Sparkle its red wine lips smacking a smile

Souls know no regret

Gender an abstract concept

Genetics breed generations.

I still remember telling dad

It is 6 feet a pyre in a public cremation ground

I am scared to be alone, can find lost souls

Could have some chat.

Till the end, he laughed on it ....but oh yeah

I do yonder 6feet ...is all and why this drama of life so

odd .why can't we laugh aloud.

6 feet is all...that matters.

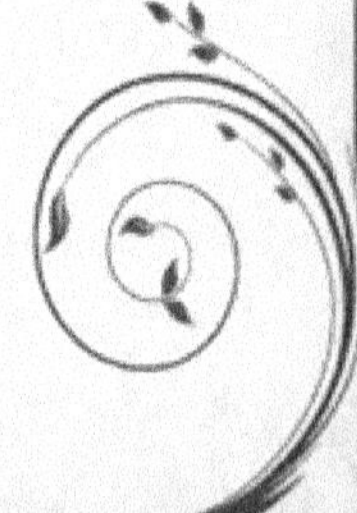

LOVE TRANSPIRED

World oh world

could you ever conspire

to mute or transmute love?

You failed each time and in the pages of history lovers

walked their path

Untrodden less traveled

yet you define love and set boundaries

dictate its rules and regulate its ways

Ignorant Vagrant proud and vain

they seldom feel it nor pine or yearn for it.

But those lost in it and consecrated in it

Dust to Dust ...Ashes to Ashes

Still, they illuminate the dark

with eyes lighten up with hope's

they are lamps themselves

and they the flame and glow

True love blooms in wounds

thrives in pain

World oh World

could you dare silence

a heart that stood for love's sake?

Desires and dreams sprouted and bled

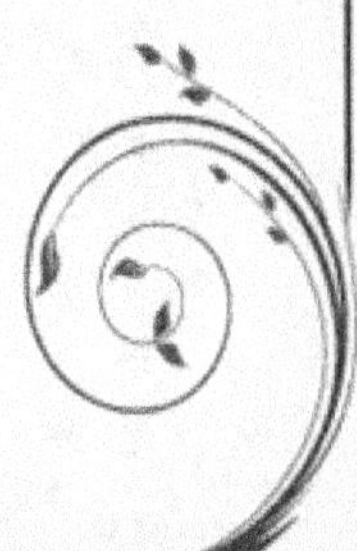

and kept it alive not withered

like branches love spread in generations and poets and

painters gave it birth and rebirth

sculptors dancers and writers nurtured it

Love became a movement on itself

World oh world

Could you ever fancy to mitigate

The love that is so selfless

Pure and serene and sanctified

It gets repeated when souls

get entangled beyond convictions and conventions.

They always become folklore and nature just admires it

and adorns such bonds

For the fire of love.

My world…is eternal and hopeful.

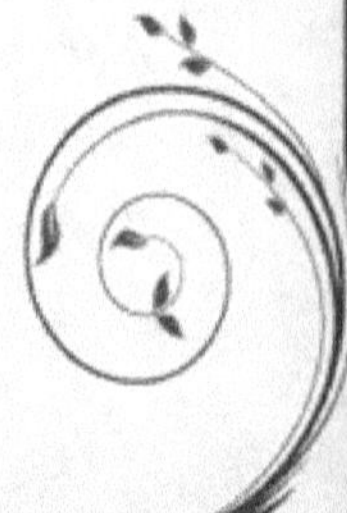

LOVE TRANSMUTED

Once sky told to the sea

give me all those deep salty pangs and pressures,

 I would pour down as pure bliss and kindle a smile as

beautiful as a rainbow in the cosmos

I would like to write an ode to you

Give me your pain and problems,

I shall find you the pleasures from the valleys of my

heart you seldom can fathom

Lend me your tears I would churn it in my soul and gift

you with Pearls of pure bliss not even the best of the

oysters can yield in such dark and doom.

Trust me with your demons I would bless you with all

Angel's that would guard all your pathways and all your

tempest like no one could bestow in the pages of past

Grant me your fears, your guilt, and your worries, poison

of rejection, deep shames, I would ingest them and kiss

your lips with a breath of life and freedom and lightness

of feather you have never fancied before

You can be as nude as truth in my arms revealing all

your scars, I would see through them the light in you and

admire your valor the way you tarried this far

You may not fear the world nor the stones of words they
throw recklessly inhuman at you I would transmute each
into verses and sing them aloud and build on your castle
for you to rule in peace the rest of your life.

You need not run away from life, I could hide you in my
core immune to the toxins and become the star that
illuminates the universe.

I am here before you shed all those wears and bearings
of yesterdays and be new creations I am your garden that
grew from the thorns world tied me to.

At this moment from the dark cocoon there rise a
butterfly and a lot of silky thread
I bind you with its freedom and blend in you as
the innocence of a dewdrop that is resting on the first
petal of unopened yet not bloomed blue lotus.

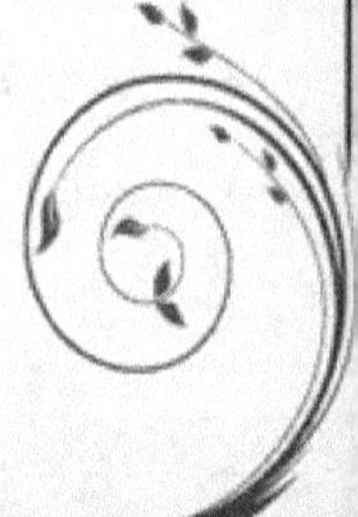

ONCE AGAIN

I wanted to walk through

the corridors of those mansions

that still could feel my heart throbs and know I wanted

to be the morning smile

that would wake them up.

In summer winter fall and snowy days

I want to hear them call me; hey, sunshine,

Want to cheer each smile open like petals

of tulips even if how bad the night went through

Make them feel there is their girl

Who can fix it all with nothing to fear

It is all taken care of; they can leave their

worries and start their routine on

my staffs, never need to fret

They don't not a boss, a friend lead on

It was a journey a team, a family

We need to bring the best out of

Whom we care and exist for

Changes yes I brought it in and around

Never cared if someone liked or not

It all went so perfect and borne fruits

Until someone put their evil eyes on it

We had celebrated all our days phenomenal

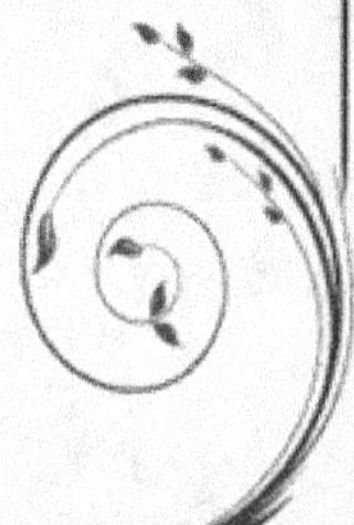

Nothing can take my place in their heart
It was not hatred that got me in to mess
It was after all love ...
I still wish I could walk down those

Corridors talk down their panic

Without restrains calm them down

I know what I am capable of

But...I left those doors broken

Lost and failed.

Framed up shattered

Still, I see those eyes that bids me good night

at late night and waits early morning

But I broke my promise to look after them

those doors are estranged to me.

Forever...for whom.it was all done

is stranger than all it and never ever turns

it is the world....how it works in this part

Western way they say.

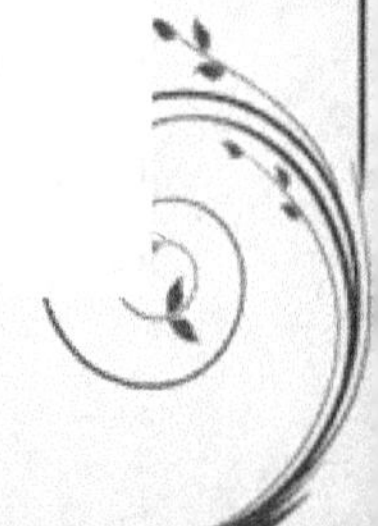

TO MY MOON

Oh my forever shining moon!!

Of these twilights of life

drenched in the night rains of my monsoons at its behest

so ardent so ravishing inviting and invading, conquering

in mesmerizing silence like petals of Rose's red

Your memories fill my eyes

with dark clouds enabling them to be luscious

with lashes reminding a thousand peacocks dancing with

rainbow in the eastern sky

There are a million doves in my heart that chirp and

quiver basking in the light sunshine

Yearning and calling forth for their pairs eternally

In the Nestle of the summer months, our passion has

gained wings like little birdies and my wild tuft of hair

arouses in you a thirst in you for a twin flame calling out

for being one in the soul.

Drops into trickles to rivulets and rivulets to marine

might

my love finds in its absolute finite in you.

In this uniqueness lies our versatility.

The way that has no replication. Isn't it worth a lifetime,

Well it is the cost

So be it.

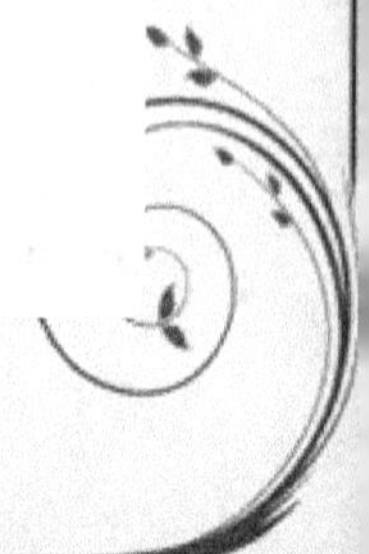

MARY OF MAGDALENE

You fascinate me

Not on who are you, I have no doubts in it however you are misinterpreted for centuries

"Apostle to the Apostle's' princess I do not want to err in depicting you.

Not at all tainting your narrative

You remain intriguing to me beautiful as a rose

The great painter never lied in it

Oh saint the cruel fate twisted your struggle

Isn't your story the repetition of the exiled feminine, of invalidation mistreatment shame, and silence.

Was it not the story of an inner Goddess that abominations erased and depicted as a whore

when you were the healer, the teacher, the influential leader who knew the God and the Son, and the spirit in your heart mind, and soul.

Oh, the Dogma of Male-dominated Semitic world would never fancy such a privilege of female arising.

You become a lamentable and disheartening pain.

For you inherited the truth of pain of the love that was crucified.

This world would have been changed by you, the lust for

power, ugly avarice, and ignorance mitigated. But you were withered

Prophecy of the arid land will you blossom again.

From where the Goddesses were burned at stake and exiled forever

will the purpose be fulfilled? Will love and harmony be restored?

Mary of Magdalene you are not a publicly defamed characterization...

You enchant me

The divine feminine!

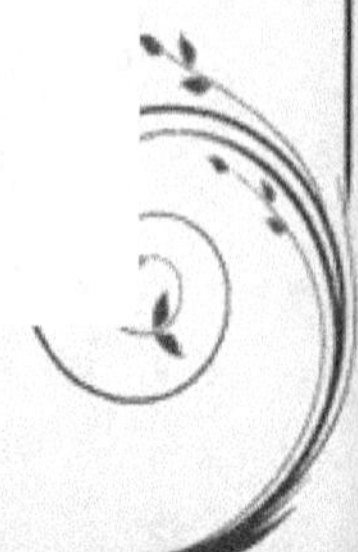

TO THE MOST UNMERCIFUL

Oh, you the unknown, unheard, unseen cloud that never

belongs to any, why did you engulf the sunshine that

offered a lifetime to burn and bestow the best for others.

You made some world's days turn dark even before it

was yet the noon and yet the divine cause was even met

Shadowless lam left alone in this pitch blackness but to

tarry barefooted on the thorns and the coral reefs.

When memories of those days seep in it causes scalded

wounds so painful.

Silence draws me into its bosom and I forget my words

I freeze as a rivulet unable to branch out or seek.

In every breeze henceforth in this land, I experience

thorny slashes embedded treacherous hidden in it and in

every stranger I meet it personifies as a trauma

In the lullaby of the birds of this land, I feel strangely

there is a note of melancholy, pain, solitude, and

estrangement. Lives here are just masks and underneath

there is unkind apathetic glare and nothing more

I still go on as a strained string of sitar that still sings

synchronized with the symphony but is broken each day

bit by bit

You, my traveler cloud, why did you just black out the

sunshine. It would have brought a lot of spring with it;

autumn monsoons, love, and light brighten many lives

with meaning.

You wiped off...sunshine

and just vanished into nowhere!!!!

I am bound wings shattered....to be sunshine

But I still kindle light like a lamp.

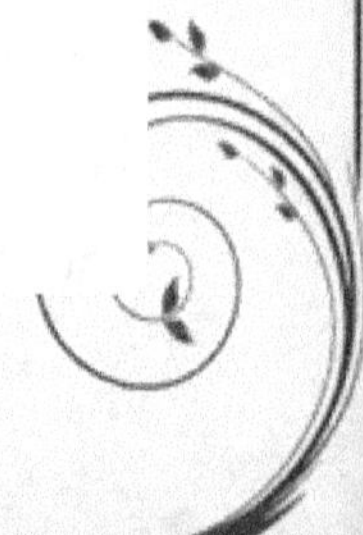

SILENT TEARS

I walk these days on earth

with a fistful of dreams and promises to fulfill.

Hope's in my aging heart not ready to give up but to do

something and be someone

Who is a lonely wolf hurt wounded but still

Battling in the pitch

How in the world will you stop me

The truth that I am and the lie that you are

Great might I ask you .....

If I cannot remove the darkness by being

The sunshine that I was, I am going to be the fire myself

and spread the light

How in the world will you hold me back

Blazing scorching I am before you

I am not a trickle, a rivulet but the real marine might and

I am not the ornamental garden orchid that you watered

and fondled to bloom

I broke the rock hearts with my roots so hard to hold on

and survived the dry deserts

My flowers are unique, for the needy less fortunate.

How can you ever fancy erasing me

Wipe me, banish me, a poem, engraved with blood on

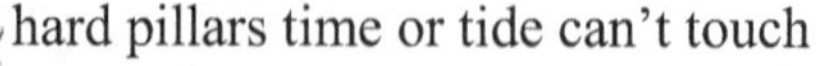

hard pillars time or tide can't touch

I am not your savvy glass collection that could break and be pushed back

I have been raised in infernos of blames defamation belittling and rejection and but nothing

So I have more strength than the cruelty you bestow you can't fathom me breaking down.

I learned to stand straight for once by stooping million times making my backbone a stepping board

I don't fear you a bit takes this from me .your insolent might too.

Your Hell of fire has brought out the best version of golden me just before universe.

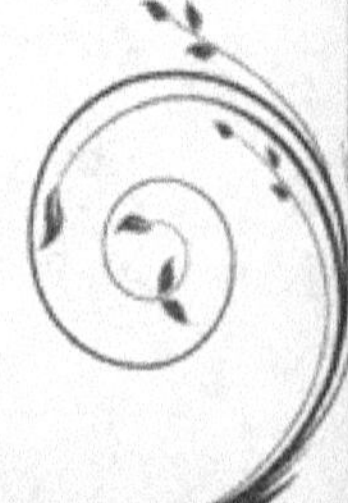

IN OUR TIMES

In our time, love had a different definition very unlike

today's

It was conceived deep in the soul like lightning and

made many earthquakes in our hearts those days

Drenching our hand towels in sweat that smelled of

sandalwood

There comes the role of friends, heated discussions

confiding and assurances murmuring of experiences

shared and advises from authentic sources

The eventful meeting takes place at a junction near the

tuition centers, the cycle bells that quivers and anklets

that tremble

It seemed all so vivid and natural the fragrance of oil on

the long black hair and the jasmine flowers on them

well-adorned making an aroma

No words were exchanged but letters written with

Reynolds pens and eyes that meet often shy away not

extending in a stare.

In our times love had a different feel the letters were

hidden in the book covers to be read in solitude mostly

when only lovers are awake in the last part of the night

with a morning star.

Read and re-read replies are written after quite an effort
in literature, fumbling books in a public library.
Those days people read books both Byron and Keats to
share beautiful words

In our times Love was unique dears

To exchange our mind through eyes

To convey passion with lips

To imply the lust with heartbeats heaving

Some ended in marriages

Some ended in crossroads

Our era would be extinct of our kind

Who wanted to bloom in some wilderness

As someone who lost in love wrote

To spread the fragrance to the air and wither away

....forever.

In our times Love...was yeah ...something different,
friends.

THE SILENCE

The silence between us

Is increasing day by day

I know I am filling my hours with gloom

And distances keep you in a hermitage of doom

Words take form between us and aborted progenies to

get sucked into cavities of eternal time cavities erasing

our togetherness in this spatial existence a reality,

denying our being

For each other a futile conviction.

Fate destiny moments nothing seemed

right for us and the bridge of conveying

Any reminisces seems broken forever

Anger is only what we save for each other

Blames and hatred for one another

Where has our love disappeared

That bled for each other when every

atom, reverberated antagonizing us

It is all matters of a lot of hurts

The world did to us and we could not refute

Why do we fear to live life to its maximum?

enjoying every bit of it

Let bygones be bygones

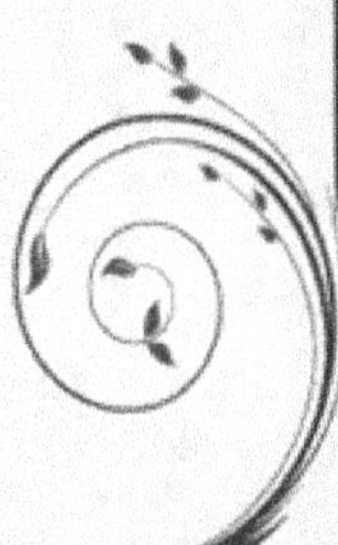

These moments are still ours

why don't we leap of faith

Forger bitterness world offered and live

A life meaningful come what may be

Why hate you and why you hate me

Let us just keep love in the heart and try bloom

spring on this earth

Let us be an inspiration

When everything is lost there is still

Hope and love

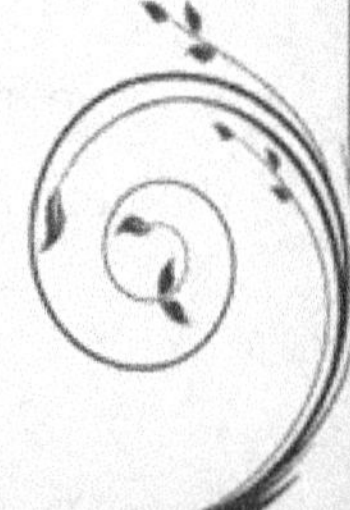

DOVER BEACH

Dover beach

I would like to be absolved in

Your mob where my face is estranged to me

I could let myself simmer in the waves

Unknown unheard disappearing to the plenitude

submerging my solitude in it

The people lost in their own havens

Basking in their own little sun and making

Their own little heaven blending with

The golden sand and their skin I never

Bothered of its texture or color

My brown skin cinnamon honey

as many described raising the

confusion of my origin which I enjoy

my piercings my tattoos my accent

Nay, I never fit in any box

I don't want to belong

I wanted to feel weightless of the clouds

I never felt bothered by the weedy aromas

It seemed natural and real every moments

The streets, the grills, and bars

The seagulls, the songs and dancers

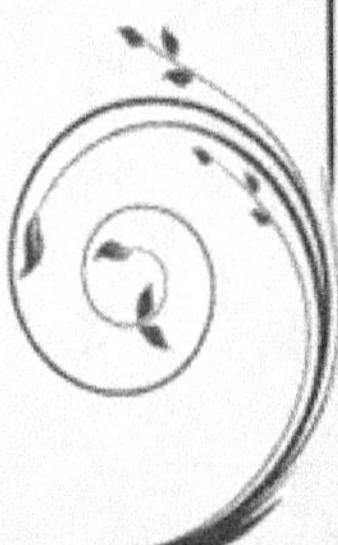

I never felt love kindled in me
The waves came and left
Hearing my pain and passion
I whispered to receding water
All I wanted is to be erased and forgotten
I just felt I am as old as those molecules
bearing untold stories in the very heart
listening to many a hearts wrenching
allowing to unwind them and taking them
making life so salty...
deep yet always bubbling up in mirth

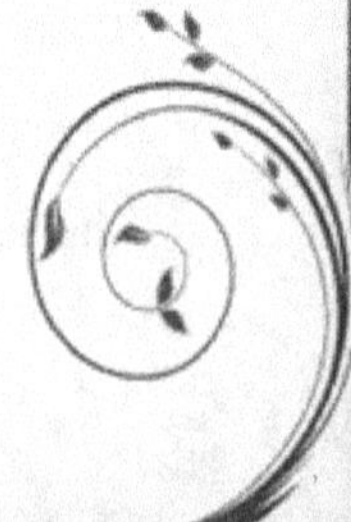

MY MINDFULNESS

On the verge of impetuous ways, days fall off, why do

you become my mindfulness

Why when every atom in my being cry out for presence

your absence and emptiness are written in golden in my

fate to accept and succumb

When you are my pride and honor why bitterness of

defamation become my elixir of existence.

When all I want is a glance of you, why did you choose

to part and in the darkness you gifted me, my love is

losing its essence and direction and it remains in me as a

passionless numbness.

In the Depth of my soul, I can feel a bird whose wings

are shattered and to strangers, I appear untamed wild,

and misfit

No, I am not going to end up as the monument of your

lost love

Sleepless nights are endless with your thoughts and you

are in my every walk and every breath

Every aims and destination and my efforts shatter and

wither like mirages in deserts in front of my eyes now.

Your loss and the pain you say you endure fill in my

veins like venom uprooting my days as well.

Come Oh great world

By distance between me and you

I am seldom shaken

I do not think you are a cheat

Nor was I a traitor

You have become so natural like a habit in me

With years

Oh dear one

With years...

FREEDOM

Break open the shackles and chains that forces you to

succumb to any atrocity

You are destined with a cause to meet

A purpose just unique drives you to end

Try to seek it out and make your mark in the world

Leave your imprints for times yet to come

Raise up your vibrations above the pity

Trivialities of common ways and be not

the subject of misery marketing but a

Hurricane that can still uproot conventions

and convictions, judge not and not allow

the cruel mob to raise their fingers in

judging you, beg no forgiveness if you

trust, you have not erred and you trust

You were right on your part and live with pride

Head high and foot to the ground never waive

Keep going don't give up you are not the

Wick of the lamp but the real Sun that

burn to enlighten every atom so fear not

when you blaze in heat and pressure

but take up your fight and be on the side

of right, trust in your gene there is Sita so

You will cross over fire and Krishna if ever your

Chastity is touched there would be a war on it.

Look at your enemy in their eyes and walk on this earth

like a queen, let love be your watchword...fret not my

mind ...

Listen...Seek thou ...thyself

In thou lies...thy success and truth.

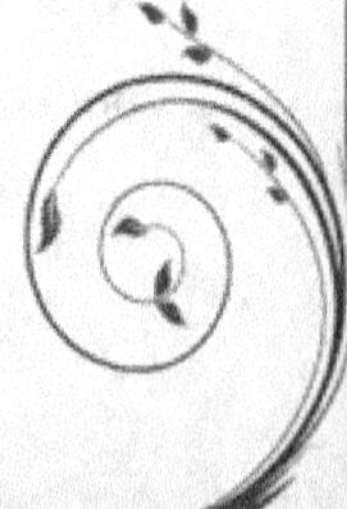

NIGHT LILIES

Like a newly half bloomed night lily that is drenched in

mist my eyes seek you

frantically my soul whispers to me.

I negate each time such remarks yet I realized you were

building in me like unexplainable mirth that filled every

vacuum in me sealing off the God-given cavities and

emptied my evening thanking in million arms

embarrassing myself ...

Is the sky playing its most heavenly notes on the strings

of rain the most ardent and divine unknown unheard

symphonies

Would it not evoke the celestial beings to fall in love

with earthlings these moments that monsoon creates at

its behest

I used to fathom when you and I met every single time.

During those times

I remember nature swelled in pleasure where rivers sang

and the canopy of bamboos swayed in an enchanting

beat calling forth numerous nameless birds to repeat it in

a choir

Like our meetings so short-lived the twilight merged into

the earth in deep ecstasy which demanded no words

The lamps in Yamuna did flow majestically like a
saffron mark encoded on the forehead of a beautiful
bride.
Yet today in the despondency of your abandonment
where you left untold unheard on the bed of arrows
society created for me with rejection dismay hatred
anger and defamation, I do not let out a cry but fight my
way. I defer by not being a picture of misery but a
celebration of love and life.
I made my palace with the stones thrown
at me. I am a poet

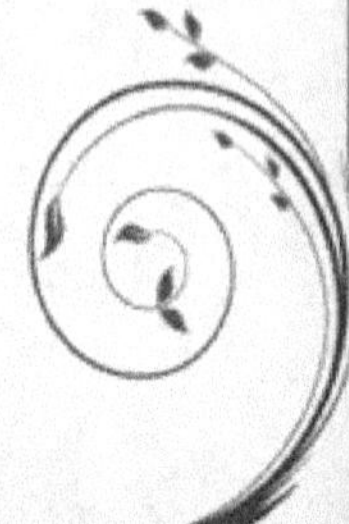

ROADS LESS TRAVELLED

Beneath the mirth and merriment

the laughter and mesmerizing

mischievous looks,

My eyes struggle in its

tantalizing gazes to hide the cruel emptiness

In the lanes of life journeyed and yet to tarried

I know those red sandal pathways leading to my

windows of memory and mind are

untrodden and less traveled

There are no signs of a traveler

still, I keep the carved wooden oak doors

half-closed half-opened

My heart...I know not yet

I stretch out my arms to feel the rain

Are the raindrops strange like the people

Do they think of color and race

Of geographical boundaries

In the twilight of life

I wear my anklets and listen to their

sounds when I look out into my courtyard

I love to feel this panging to wait upon

The hope it kindled the smile it renders

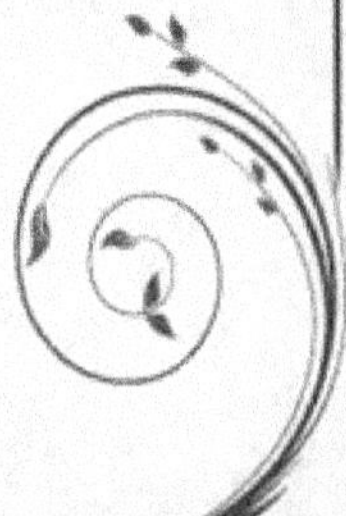

I know no one had promised to return

When they left my world and no one

Has committed a lifetime long

But still when the old clock struck

I feel someone is on the way

Am I an orchard for autumn and summer

Monsoon and winter

Spring comes as a traveler who lost his way

And return fast without a word

Why is this written in my book of fate

That I am an Inn not a home

But as every day and days to come and go

without complaint like those night lilies

Who has a lifetime of a night to bloom

And doom, my eyes look out long away

In to the path for that soul mate

Who would walk in

When I know the road is less traveled

I am an untrodden path that seldom

Could be chosen...

I know ....still I keep the oak doors half

Open half-closed.

IN YOUR ABODE

In your abode with your aroma

Filling my evenings and your keen eyes and ears

awaiting my rendering of rhapsodies

I composed or yet to compose

I still fumble for words, similes

Verbatims and intricacies of poetry

Seems very alien to me and I lose

My self before you beyond convictions

Your smile tranquilize me

Mesmerizing me with your enchanting

A glare that seeps into the soul

What do I recite

To keep ramble on love

I am seldom a teenager

Yet like an occimum Santalum in rain

I feel so enticed in love

Like a sitar whose strings are reverberating

In heavenly notes I vibe

To cry out on my lose

That our life is just two parallel Ray's

Never to blend but travel together

And meet and perish in infinity

I am not naive, I am strong
To stand the pain
Not to lament on me and you.
When you just fill my face in your arms
Look into it to see your reflection
I could sing a lot of prosodies
That could tell you of me and my
love that is like a rainbow that can
create ripples of peacock feathers in you
In your abode with lamps lighten
Jasmine's blooming around
I can become your best poem.
You ever had written or heard

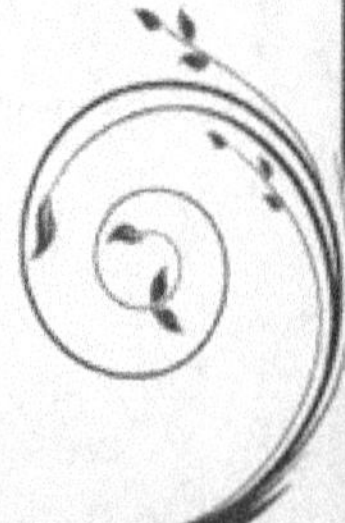

MY COVID-19 DAYS

In those times Covidien days

Beneath my masked face

I hold my tears from flowing

Sucking it up, keeping a smile

I perform the great art of instilling

Life, fighting a fight that worth it

Feeling the stench of perilous air that

is betraying freezing the moments

Of this outbreak, but I wrestle

With chances and racketing

the flux that taunts to valor

at the time saving a couple

Of life even if mine is in hazardous

quirk I don't care.

It is the fellow being wincing

in agony sprawling for breath

and I just not need to be a hero

nor a frontline but to do what I

am capable of spreading

Love and light of my great nation

This havoc rare rumpus

It took meek and proud with no regard

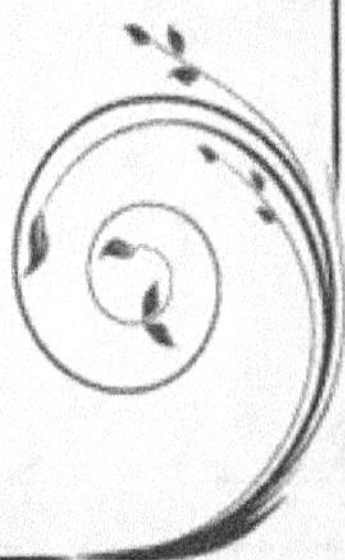

I know it is no time to bargain

Ransacked I am in my oppressor's eye

I did not count the breaths I brought back to life, nor

lives I saved

I did not tell my name

Just walked away

In the time of crisis, it is true ....Angels come ...

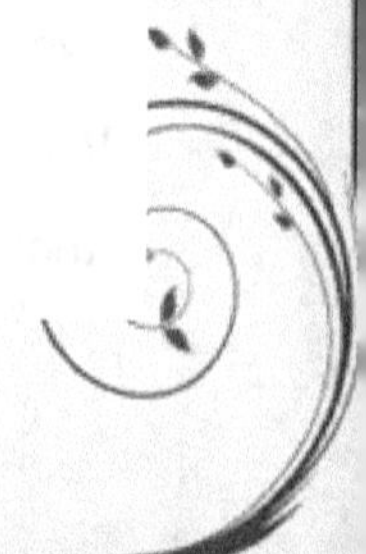

TO MY LOVE

Drizzle shower engulf, entice enthrall and embalm me

as the first hail storm did to me

In my eyes that are deeply dark and dense like

wild grapes floating in oceans of desires and hopes glow

burning serene,

fill up their contours and curves with those inks that

maketh their art eternally loveable.

Like a rainbow of seven colors be engraved on my heart,

with all those meshes let me portray your face in the

depth of my sublimed sanity

I follow your soul in the lanes of unknown terrain of day

and night

and you become the canvas of vastness for my endless

passions and thoughts to manifest

In your presence, I feel the lightness of a feather that

could float the whole night speaking endlessly on beauty

and happiness like the winter fingertips that solicitly

touches

a leaflet that readily gives way to falling into selfless

bliss of complete submission and surrendering.

When you gently kissed on my forehead with

care compassion and honor that never failed

I shuddered and quivered in sentiment that lack

deciphering

Let us awaken in it as a unique oneness

We are an ardent passion that keeps the flame alive and

on

Again Drizzle shower and storm unto me

In those glaciers let me remain as a sculpture that

admires you till eternity until I am excavated and my

story been told

Let me be buried with an untold, unwritten tale of ours.

VERSES, MY VERSES

Verses my very verses

Don't they evoke you

With an invisible gentle touch on

the strings of your heart my love of life

like one of those snowy ardent nights

Where did a lonely nightingale sing

When did the most beautiful rose open

Sepal and petal so swiftly and smoothly

Giving way to the single dewdrop

Making a melody that is unfathomable

Leaving nature exploding in unexplainable ecstasy that

words can never do comprehend

And our pain transpiring into a great passion

Won't you, my love. Ever reverberate

Reciprocate in the same symphony

The ocean unwinding into a sweet slumber

Submerging the sun unto her bosom

Like the most precious pearl like a maiden

newlywed would wear in her pride

Does she fancy the face of her Sun

that raise and set burning her days and nights

I just smiled to myself unable to decipher

what kindled it on my lips I yonder

the saffron skies maketh the blemishes

and blushes that are contagious and

radiant as though I too share the divine

love that knits nature and nurtures it

my beloved.

My love my verses

Don't they speak to you of me

when the waves form a thousand

peacock feather layers below and sky forms

red collages of patterns that collide.

When the Day merge into the arms of nights

in a complete surrender

My paintings find their meaning in your eyes

My soul, I let loose in your arms

like the unbounded pastures of bliss

and in you, my finite is well encompassed

My verses

Don't they converse with you

in silence in-depth in the infinity of eternity.

I am mesmerized!!

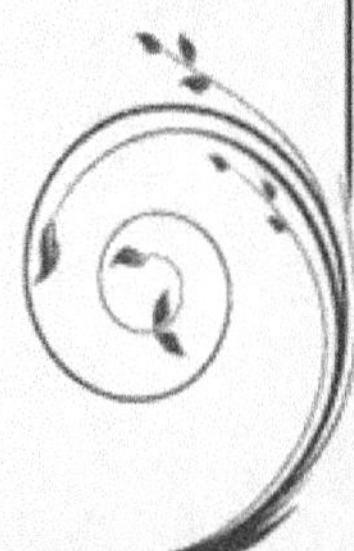

MY MIDSUMMER EVES THIRST

My midsummer eves thirst

your monsoons at its behest

with all its passion the northeastern

winds can bring forth to tropical evergreen plains.

Let these moments pass on as sumptuous

revealing every spell and speck its magic

Every drop mingle amalgamate into each other

It is forever we are conversing to each other

It never could find a finite completion

A little more, nay it is just infinity

It is not easy to define me

nor you and our coexistence

It is not as easy to walk the path of love

It is not everyone's cup of tea

To burn and enlighten like stars

To give away the self and perish

Like flowers, but still, lovers set forth

Like fireflies and dewdrops, they rise

and fall, some write their few verses

Some sing, some get lost and vanish

Shall we walk a bit long as it was always

My question, your smile was the answer

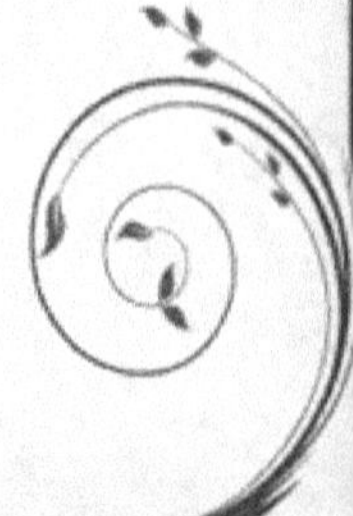

Those memories lanes ardent and red with

Some unknown floral patterns

The monsoon, the yellow canopy of blossoms

That always flowered at the wrong times

Like endless pairs who walked their ways

beneath hand in hand, the days I learned

death has a fragrance rather than a pungent aroma

which I always reminisced since then as a professional

gift ......

You...the empty teacups ...my dreams

my endless dreams that perished in

Monsoons or tears Know I not...

Let these moments pass on.

It is the eve of life...

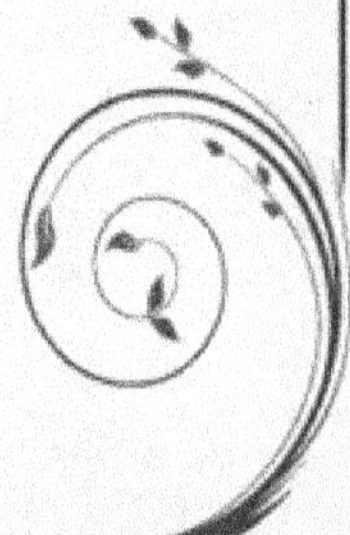

LOVE IS NEVER A BLASPHEMY

If ever want to turn to me

I am not an epitome of self-pity and if ever someone has

to share their heaps of advice

Sorry, you have no damn idea of what is my mess and

What are personal devils I fight

day today, so stay out of my hell of a business.

I am sober yes leave me to grieve the deception of

people, systems, and nation and my friends and foes.

People in sobriety are disgraceful and crazy do forgive

mine too.

Do not look into my eyes, read my soul. Let my share of

pain die along with me.

I did not come to this land on my accord and I am not

leaving that way.

I will strive to reach my success. This poem I did not

plan it.

Among the disguises in the very land, I have not met a

true individual.

I do not miss my country anymore but.

People in this land use us like in a chess game. I am not a pawn anymore.

I wowed to be queen.

I don't understand this place anymore. I am a drop of dew in this ocean. Will I be alive a day?
I was a moth to fly to this candle.

What can save me?

Spiritual emptiness eats you day by day. But Yeah I am a poet .a lover. Inside a lover's heart, there is another world

There is a lake inside me of what I am, searching outside.
I see barriers ...
Let me focus on abundance beyond it in all my pain and losses.
I still do not know this land. I am trying to find my place in this emptiness.
Bewildered why this happened
But I will live it...m not pity partying
I enjoy this challenge and defamation.
Love is never a blasphemy.

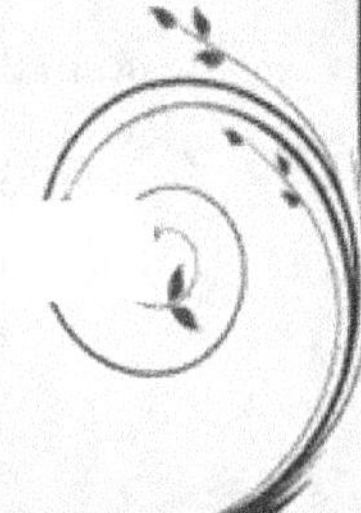

MY PRIDE

I take that pride

In being the woman

You never could get out of

Your insolent imperial ostentatious head

Which had a nerve audacity and vanity

That overpowered a frail heart

That missed a beat every time my name

Was taken by strangers and struggled

To conceal the pangs of unknown

Possessiveness you denied

Every single day

I still smile

In being that woman

You can't resist to keep loving

As you know the generosity of an ocean in

my love where you experience the freedom

of a fish never confining

But you resist it and fight

abandoned fights

no matter you fail

You know it is your rest

and fort of trust

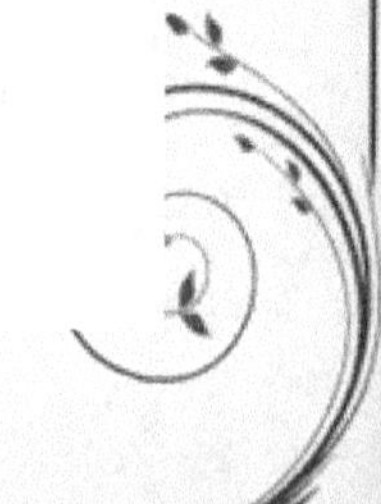

Your earth and rock

I love being the woman I am

because In love

I don't need your confirmation

affirmations to flourish and bloom

Like the innocence of the jasmine

Like the passion of Rose's

Like the beauty of the marigold

It happens naturally

Everything in me

The summer spring monsoon autumn

Nobody whispers to nature

I too manifest in deep ecstasy

Your very essence conspire me through

Your soul

I am contented

I know my place in your life

The Altar is beyond and above

I rest with all your heartfelt prayers

It is all right.

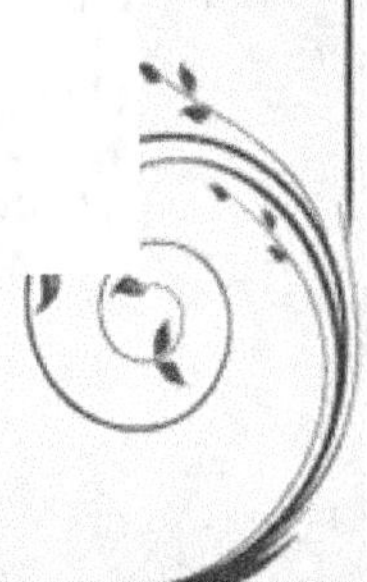

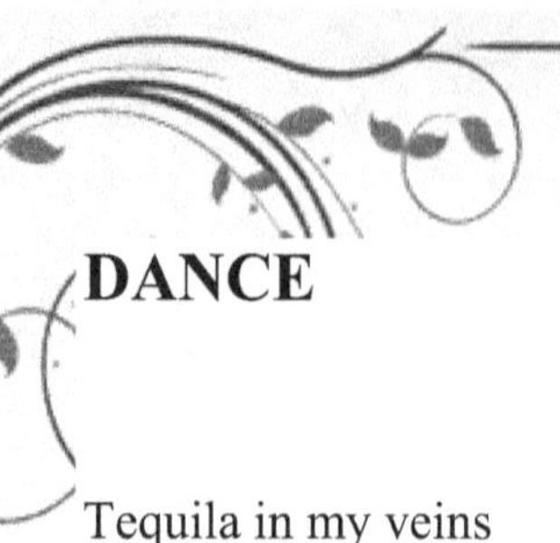

DANCE

Tequila in my veins

Flamingo in my steps

This night I want to dance alone

With abyss

The drums let it make its symphony with

My heart and I would take each step

With the rhythm of the sea

Hey you,

My gypsy old soul knight

Don't shy away this night

Is only that we have

Let us make the choir with the rain

and play with thunderbolts so wild

sway on with each whirlwind my

hips decipher oh my old friend

Before the margarita sweep us in a tide

let us kiss open the Rose's that are yet to

bloom for the day

Fill me with dreams of stardust

That I forget my pain in a shot secure

I want to sing for you the most ardent

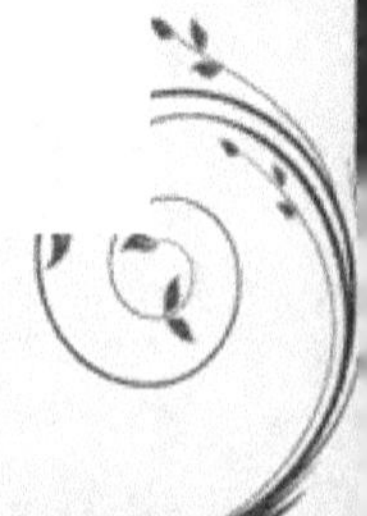

Songs oh my alchemist

The song that turns all sorrows

Great fun for future ahead

I need to dance this whole night

My hair making curls everywhere

I am not alone

The nature in its all blossom

Is with then, why need to fret

Yes my right eye my friends has scooped out

My left eye my so-called relatives

I am blindfolded and deception is all I

 got in my account, not a penny more

All whom I trusted ditched me

So gladly before sunrise, they said they do not know me.

Me and my cross are alone

Oh yes...the cross and the God

Still, I wonder why doesn't he...forsake me

In good times you are adored and worshipped

In bad times people just walk away

But God just doesn't give up...

Good or bad

I need to dance this night ...

Round across the fire

my anklets go high.

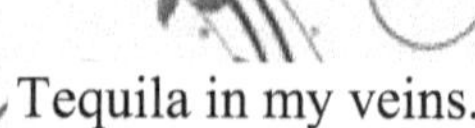

Tequila in my veins.

I need to dance to the drums of the heart

Dance of the ancients.

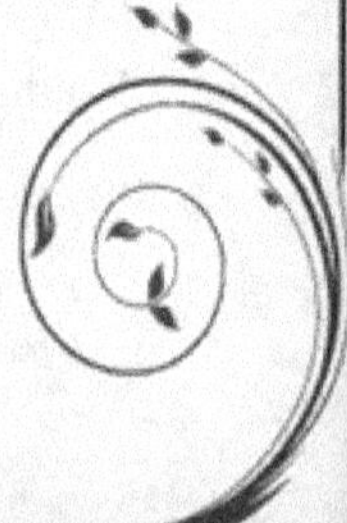

WHAT AM I

What am I
Society I seek an interpretation
I can be your canvas and your
Caricature but I yonder and ponder
This being called me and my kind
Before being born a revelation of X and Y
could erase me totally denying an expression
If born my chances of survival are half
Percentage at the mercy of being drowned
In a holy bowl of milk or a certain poisonous fruit.in any
case, I would be a disaster to the
Womb that conceived me.
Oh yeah the same womb...Gods do select
To reincarnate or be a virgin to conceive
The divinity what so ever
My kind are worshipped
My kind is enslaved
I know not what makes the difference
I can be your morning light
I can be your evening's delight
My body is exalted celebrated by poets
Artists and media

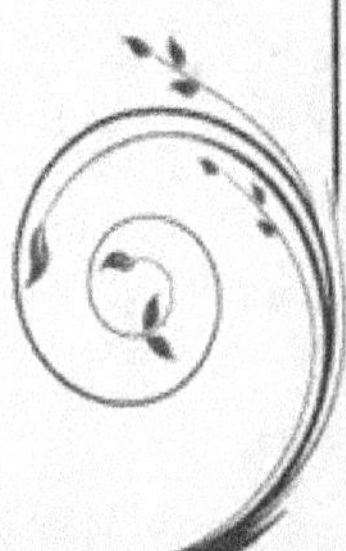

My body is a curse I am taught from childhood

From dirty looks making me crumble

When Varies told the world out her genitals

Were mutilated so that she never feels

No pleasure for women are culpable

A religion taught, no single little finger

Moved for her ...not even a women

Supported her.

When Nirbhaya was brutally violated

I still hear some say why did she go out

In the odd hours ....so callously

For abuse of my kind

There are no geographical boundaries

Like COVID-19 it is viral but nobody

Treats it as anything of value

I know when I quote this

I will be a feminist

Banking for women issues

But when will it stop this

Issues men so that women

Will stop quoting this

Six-month-old baby lay lifeless

Sixty-year grandmother broke down

Thirteen years hanged herself

A twelve year lost life in giving birth
Rescue shelters have a hundred other stories to add I
can't write down it all the way

Father brother uncle neighbor

Husband In -law ...oh ...I have been a guard

To lost minds too. So don't debate my friend

my verses are magma

I am the very earth that boil.

I am a woman

One of my kind

I will raise my voice as long as

My kind suffer on this plane

So I still ask What am I

Am I the cosmic power

That manifest the creation

Or the seven-year-old sold in sex racket

TO VENICE

This is an old story

Old as an oak tree

How do I know this

Venice tells me this when I sleep on her lap

Her green rosary cold against my cheek

Her wine smells so sweet

She rocks on her chair

Until I go to sleep

She says to me of the land

Were green pastures laid on

Every house looked great like mansions

And those women with blushing faces

She too waited for the war to end

Her man to return

She was young

Beautiful

Venice, Venice when I fall asleep

Don't you go I make her promise

her pregnant uterus moves and

We feel the baby nudge

He is got to be a handful girl

Can I have him Venice

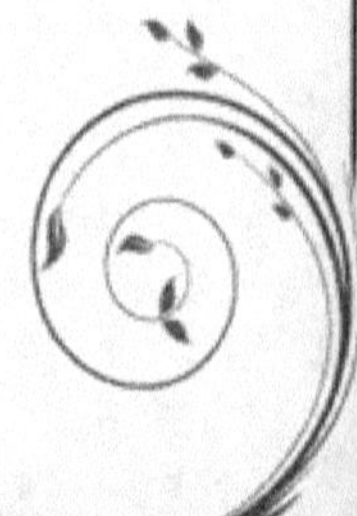

My pretty child ...this one is a mess

But when he needs me ever

Be there for him

He will feel me in your love

My care and never feel alone

You are his armor, my child

Never forsake him, pretty girl

Saying this she put me to sleep

The Irish Celtic cross stay beneath my

Pillow and I still say the rosary beads

it was our secret. No one ever knew it

When the world broke me vilify and calumniate me to

core

Venice just held me close to heart

Her son yes a handful a pain was he

But she treads me through the thorns

always knew I was messed up

Wounded yet upholding my virtues

Shattered but fighting for that pact

I and she shared all the way

Alas!!

Venice I am on my knees

What can I do

I don't know honey

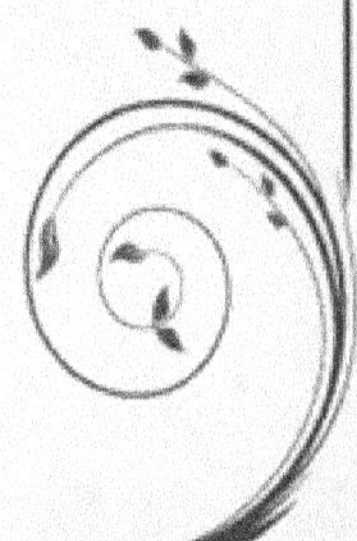

My mom...I dare call you so

I did all I can

You know I am withered ...I let go

Venice my every piece can't hold your pieces

Together it is the truth ...the story always not end

happily ever as you read on

Lady ....but there is no ray of hope in clouds.

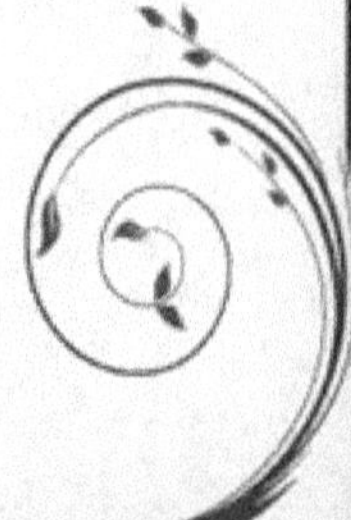

OUR CHRONICLE

How can we narrate this

Chronicle of ours.....ah yes

Ours the ignominious the opprobrious

relationship discredited in the pages of

yesterday, you nor I, giving a damn

Care and living our life in two divergent

Contrasting life busy running three leg races

With time and nemesis preordained.

Stoically ...

But why our chemistry,

the broken me finds its eternity

in the broken you and nothing

There is no need for language space-time

needed in this merging

The cold insecurities in me

find warmth in your insecurities

and it nullifies forever

I know this world has berated me

belittled you and played games

Where we were checkmates

Your disheveled shattered existence

completes my inner wounds.

You could just get lost in my arms,

keep away the chauvinism and cry

I could just find my lost sleep

And for hours find my sanity

We exist as

mystical Magical and Miraculous

deep secrets of the earth

that sprouts with certain Rain

We ignite in souls as a fire

that only disseminate the light

How long would we remain

Silent before this candle

The first snow of my winter

I still do remember in these midsummer days

To confess to confine to conceal

We still...are there

The not giving up you

The never downtrodden me

We made a team

It is good to know....this chemistry of ours

Buddy

This love of ours

Sacred sanctified serene

Not asking any favors each other

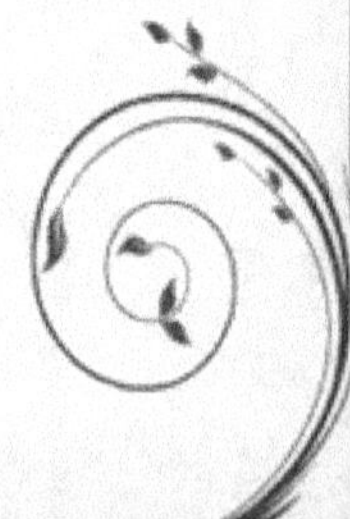

Let it be ...Timeless boundless
Nudity of our soul don't
Need an explanation for it.
It is freedom ...so it be

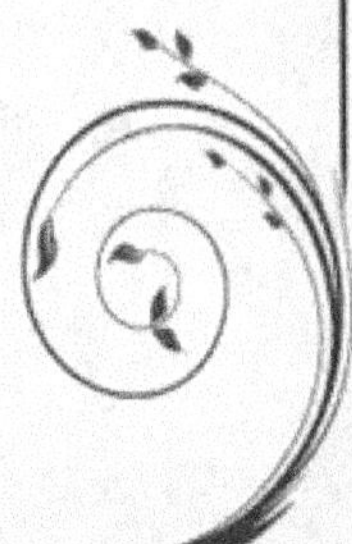

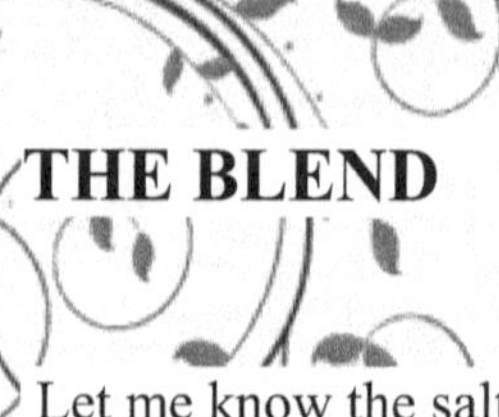

THE BLEND

Let me know the saltiness
Of the sea until
My tears are blended in its
Vastness and I be replenished by
the old souls that guard the matter
Sublime be my passions that
I don't contain them anymore
I vaporize and pour out and drench
Seep and sprout as cycles
Far apart from the rows of marshaled
Civilizations bloom and perish
Kingdoms that beguile and crumble
Life seems a tide of alluding wonder
Tranquil in moments and a catastrophe
When trying to repose, never leaving
a chance to comprehend the nectar
Just to gulp it down and be with it
Never letting go nor owning it
Was it a failure to adorn the
Robe of an obsequious angel after all
the efforts, nor did gain the love of life
Still, I exist at my soul's liberty

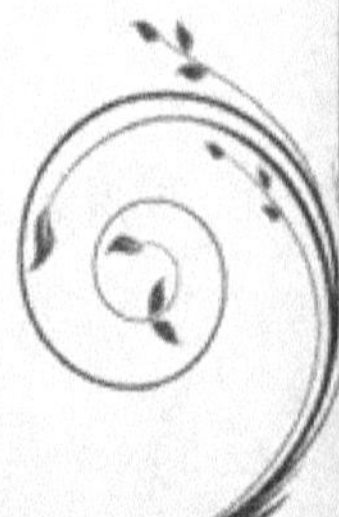

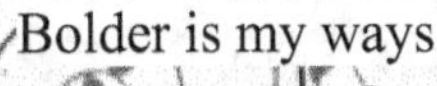

Bolder is my ways

Imperial my pride

The treacherous past peeps in as an

apparition but I win

My heart is in a dialogue between

God and death

Vice and Virtues

Cold and Heat

Dark and Light

Night lilies open their petals

In the pitch darkness

The fragrance, you, and a cup of wine

My book and this pen

Let me write to eternity some beautiful lines

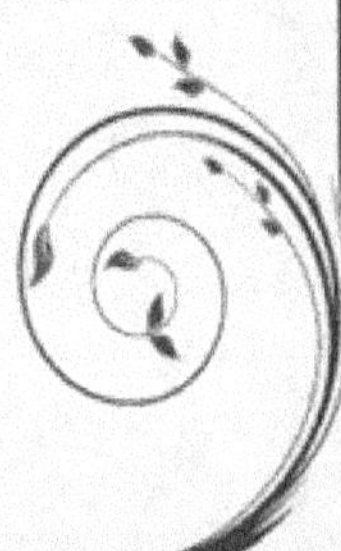

NOBODY COMMITS A SUICIDE

Nobody commits a suicide

Single-handed it is a murder

In disguise, behind every act

Of self-harm, there will be enemies

hiding who can't abuse physically

So they hurt a person mentally

So bad and heinous that soul

Would want to leave the body

Not taking back a look

Such cold-blooded is suicide

Let it not go unnoticed

Behind every suicide

There are a million dreams shattered

A heart so badly rejected

Broken for no reason than treason

A job seized from someone

Wings cut off brutally

And asked to fly miles in light-years

Yeah it is true such people

They may be self-made sensitive ones

They would have come from earth's innocence

They won't be crooks nor gossipers

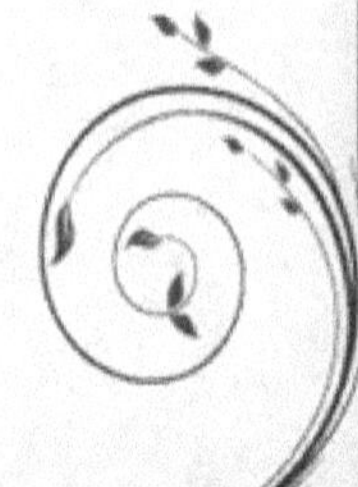

They won't be part of any filth

And would be called vulnerable

So easy to term it and forget it

For its own sake society

But nobody ever dies by themselves

There is a murderer behind them

Some kill the body but some

Very cleverer ones

Kills the mind so artistically

And call itself harm....suicide.

ME THE ETERNAL LOVE

Me the Eternal love

I do not need a definition

Any more nonetheless

I am the love

In this cosmos trying endlessly

To consume itself

I do my single-minded quest for my beloved

My iconoclast may differ

I am not confined to a pigeonholed self

But I live my life burning like

A camphor day by day

Reforming into a new reality

What did I see in you

Your flute soothes my soul.

Your single touch revives my being

No mundane accomplishments

Of versatile erudition stands

Between me and you

No time no spatial existence

We merge into one

Do you see in those flowers

Of red Indian tulips my lips

Searching for a divine passion

You close it with a syllable

My eyes which sparkle in tears

You kiss them open

You do to them

What sun rays do to lotus

In your hold my diamond

Waist ring broke and its bells

Make the seven ragas as though

On a brilliant sitar with your

Handsome long fingers

I become your music

The instrument and when you

Took my feet in your arms

My lord adorned them with

Henna scribbling with peacock

Feather triggering every nerve

In me throbbing to giveaway in ecstasy

Your humble love made my anklets

Shy away in vanity

To possess and to give up

I felt the irony

My love felt complete

And found its meaning in its

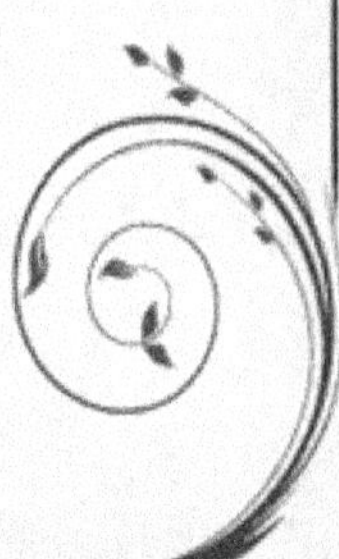

Higher purpose

It is years generations yoga

I wait for you

Never feeling hopeless

My love for you increases

Exponentially day by day

I testified by this separation

But at the shore of Yamuna

Sat Radha ....Epitome of Eternal love.

Tears flowing down in bliss

Remembering her God and Lord.

As though suffering was necessary to

Embellish a valuable lesson

the lesson of eternal love.

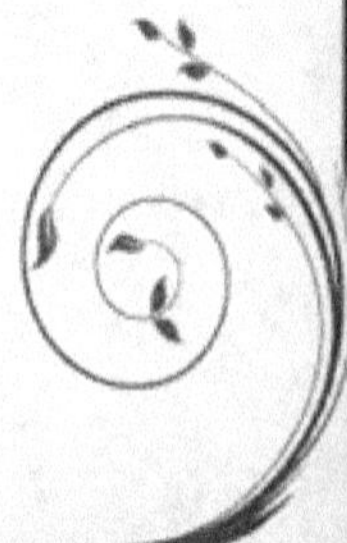

THEM AND ME

Them and me

When I could relate

Loss in the concrete world

And understand abstract

I was four just four and nothing more

There starts my journey with them

The language was no barrier I was trained

They came to my home as people

I believed who shared their world with me

When Gandhi told me his experiments with

Truth I knew Annie Frank had a diary

Where she portrayed a period

I could barely imagine and still

Learned words can heal and words

Are friends in doom and gloom

At eleven when my uncle handed

Me his copies of Tale of two cities

And three musketeers, I know not

Still, he feels the same about me

You can, I said I don't understand

He said listen to the characters

Look into dictionaries but read

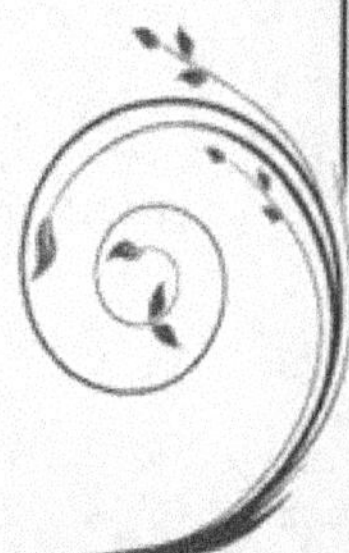

I did and feel a love for the lawyer in it

And knew what revolution means

Dickens to Chekov I stumbled and struggled

But dad always in his pain talked

Changampuzha and Idapalli

So I learned people can

Pour their pain in verses

My aunts my cousins

Most of them filled

my little world

with stories and their authors

I can't coin it all out

I was nerdy Bratt

Was I

Don't think so

Then came adolescence

And there started my conflict of interests

A friend who slid My story

Opened my world to a new horizon

I was looking into a mirror

I loved the way She wrote

She became a passion and equation

Kamala Das, there started my rebellion

Or maybe before

I could not say, Asha poorna Devi

I shall not defy Prathiba Rai

I would never adore but Arundhathi Rai

I never could make sense in her writings

Well I would say, Sara Joseph

But it never stopped there

A room I have filled with books

I don't live there anymore

Where I landed up

I made another

But I had my own

Quite a few

I wished to learn Literature wanted

To ponder Shakespearean arts

Had a yearning to get lost in stoic words

Even planned my thesis on Sylvia Plath

What am I doing now...

I miss Nanditha at times

Think a lot about Pablo Neroda

Very much feel what in the world

Balachandran chullikadu is doing now

Of the social media writers

I enjoy all write-ups

Think ...old man and sea

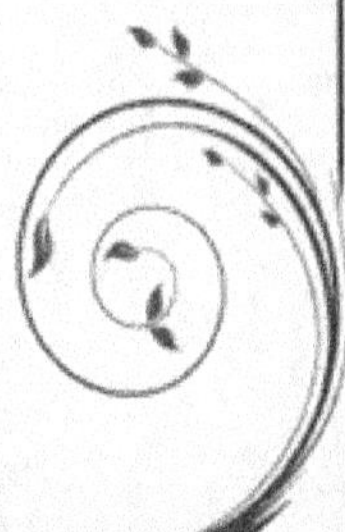

Writers are born with signature

Of God on their heart

Many are losers

Broken souls ...yet they love the world

It is their passion that runs

Fervently as ink

Their bleeding soul-making imprints on paper.

TWILIGHT

Twilight

He reminded me it is

This eve that makes me

Ravishing ardent and exotic

And he wanted to bask in the twilight

He felt my eyes with their innocence

Curious peering black lotuses

Every time they collided with his

They smiled he presumed in ecstasy

My lips were parted petals

He fathomed of morning Rose's

That bloomed with dew drops

Still enchantingly studded

Which were conversing with him

In my deep silences

My wild hairs were tropical climbers

That made waveforms in the air

Lashing against my cheeks

That blushed he said in his presence

He said my heaving bosom

Were never lofty but raised

In pride and my hips swayed

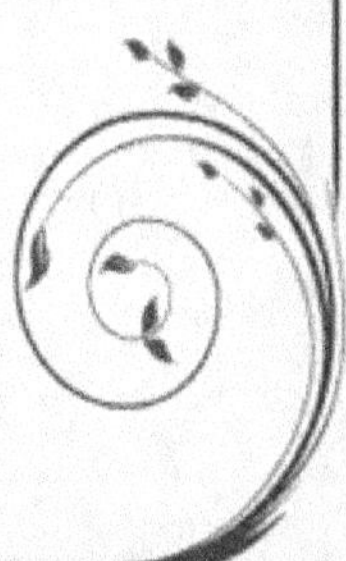

With a gentleness so womanly

Inch by inch Well crafted.

Nothing more that was how he defined.

I heard it all and just laughed

Laughter I could not stop

He must be a man every woman

Would dream of but not me

I have nothing with it ....the me

The broken crumbled me

My sun is setting on the horizon

I am just a lonely path

A road less traveled

All I have is wounds all over my heart

Wounds of treachery

Wounds of rejection

I am just a page in a book

Forgotten and Forbidden

I just touched his shoulder

Son, there are a lot of bushes

In the orchards that just bloomed

Some yet to bloom and flourish

When tired and need to tell

A story find this old

Oaktree

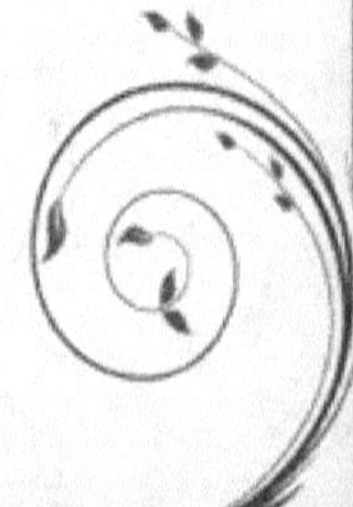

He just held my hand

What a thing of beauty

With such a depth of an ocean

Oh yes I told

The ocean holds a thousand

Secrets from time immemorial

There is a way the world is

I told...lad

While I just walked towards

My destiny.

It is the eve of life, the heart is like the sky

Clear and conscience pure

Just like a Tulsi leaflet

I wished my lords feet

Like a Tulsi leaflet

I wished my Lord's feet

Beyond the veils of like and lust

I have placed myself in a love that is

Ardent like a prayer

And it has just one aim and means

It waiver not and is still.

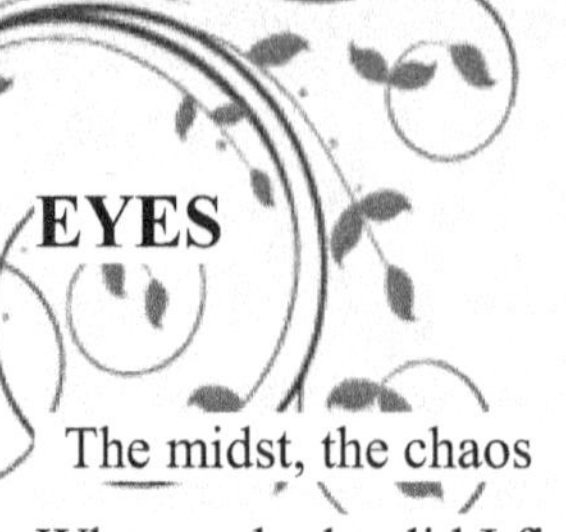

EYES

The midst, the chaos

When and why did I find my

Tranquility in those eyes

The deep eyes like the depth of the sea

Which sells dreams and sweet dreams

You never wanted to wake up from

Like the fairy tales

It opens a new world

Every look in it anoints you more

In to a heaven

It is the peace, it is bliss

It is solace it is stillness

It is all I ever wanted

But where do I seek

Those pair of pristine eyes

It makes me feel lighter than a feather

I wait and ache, I know there are thoughts

Those never find a shore

It floats in the free sky of memory

Nobody to own it or honor

I just keep asking to the horizon

Where are you

That which evanescence before

I could hold on

I yonder you in the knowledge

You are not there

I search you in mysticism

You are not there

I ponder you in the wise words

You are not there

In nature in a matter in every known unknown

You are not there

You who mesmerized me with those

Twinkling pair of jewels

I cry unto you

I need to gaze into them

To find my ultimate rest

I need to leave them

The last imprints of my existence

I felt those eyes

Paired with mine

Entangled so ardently as ever

Inseparable I closed my eyes

To find them right under my

Dark blue lotus eyes as a duality

Ending in oneness

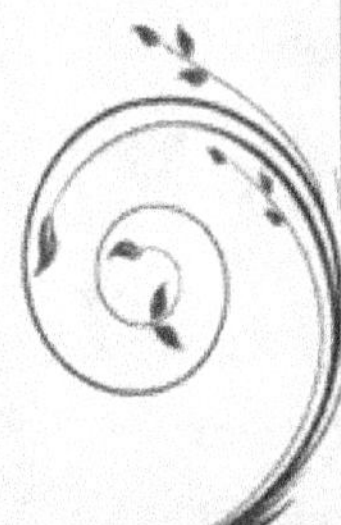

I stopped searching them outside
In me, my love found its
Tranquility and I trusted it.

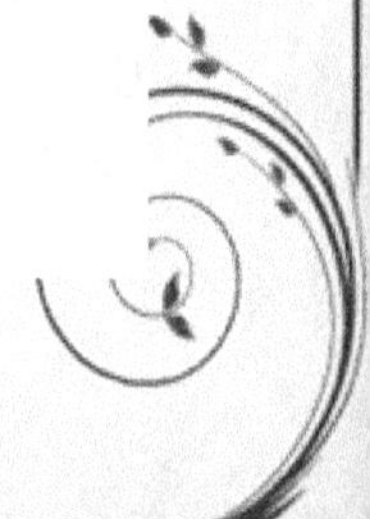

MY NATION

My nation is the abode of civilization is the alma-Mata

of culture is the embodiment of virtues

My country the great Indian peninsula

Stands out statuary of everything that is

Serene pure sanctified and Valour

Noble is its intention and poises its way

Powerful like a Lion guarding and Vigilant like an Eagle

we excel in every single field

But humble is our people.

Yet not to be stoned to death!!

I found a million souls lamenting

On the suicide of an actor

Why society just callously

You show tight-lipped silence

When our soldiers

Were brutally murdered

A soldier's death has become a casual thing to us, a

nurses death a police man's death

These are just could be, would be to us

They deserved a better death

Could have been a bullet instead of this animosity to kill

inch by inch

But this prodigious act of a neighbor nation

I pity them and condemn them

Wish them to live as dark face

Ponderous and despair on earth

They don't even deserve a death our soldiers

They were awake at boarders

When you and me, we were asleep

What did China gain

By opening up such plagued wounds

Our motto of ahimsa is not our

Pattern to succumb to atrocities

Gone are the days when India

was in deep slumber and would

Reciprocate and eye for an eye

and a tooth for a tooth.

Our soldiers don't just die

their death is martyrdom

It is a sacrifice to the motherland

we are sensitive ...yes to that.

A PRAYER

It is a prayer

Like a whisper to the cosmos

From him and me

Together ardent from our soul

Miles apart we are

World and its only beholder

The merciful of mercy

Beyond our tortured breath and tormented

Existence at this dusk of a lifetime

Write our love in the book of life tomorrow

To come

As the unwritten morning of faith sprouting

which is unshaken by locale

Not taken by time and tides

Our love until eternity burnt in itself

Transforming to stars

To guide lost souls and helpless beings

Emanating rays of milky enlightened paths

And we in a sweet embrace in that very thought

meltdown in each other's arm

This moment is now

Tomorrow is not ours

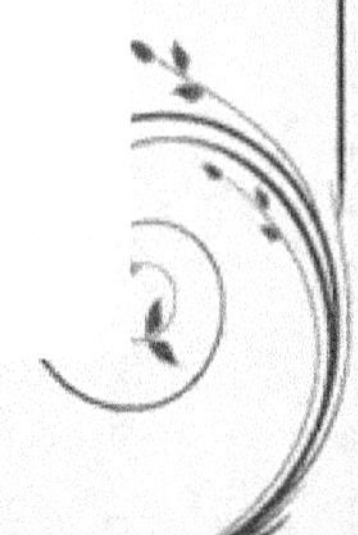

If it is not in destiny to have you in my life

Will fight with all might to rewrite the destiny

Will change lines in our palms

Every card in our deck

It is true but my dearest

That if breath exist and heart fervently bleeds

Beyond all tribulations

We are going to exist...

THE GREAT I AM TALKS

The Great I am talks

I do not know how many must have listened but he talks

He or she what would I say white or black

East or West

The Great I am and me just us

Beyond that, I can't describe

My poetic illustrations fail and I am just

Spellbound in this narrative

Because this is our private moments

In the despondency of ultimate breaking down

I felt his arms around me

Right amidst the portion I am working on

My goggles can conceal my tears

My mask my heavens and trembling lips

My mind arouses with tides

Like pull from moon pulsating in it

What do I lack

Why am I always in the art of living

A runner up when all the hard work is mine

My heart was pumping bleeding my pain

Gulping the terror I cannot let out

Why am I just an option a choice

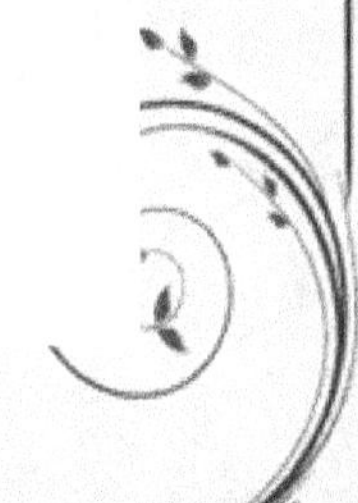

Never a destination but means

Why it happens all the time

And keeps repeating

I just did my project with a light-years speed

Fascinating people around me

No one could fathom it is the doom from deep

That is pouring out

Denial of the very truth

That someone could soullessly say

Trample over and over

And I could just be a witness

Of my own torture my trial

My tribulation and do nothing

But just take it and keep a smile on

What is my story why me in the tempest

What do I lack

Am I your mistake Oh lord

That you just went wrong by any chance

Is there a way to mend it

Great I am just said

Look into my eyes

I just peered into it

I do not make a mistake

You do not lack but have much more

That I am possessive on you

I said just cut that crap

You are just God...me...just woman

That too in midlife crisis

He said look at you

I just did so majestically and You just belong

To me

I said it can't be so

He said why it can't be so

That you write on love, you sing of love

You beg to love and just get a smitten woman

And I love you, you don't care that a bit

Why can't life a bit easy like that

The Great I am

Could fall in love I learned

Trust me I don't booze it is for real

I heard his, and I stopped worrying

What I do lack any more

That why am an option.

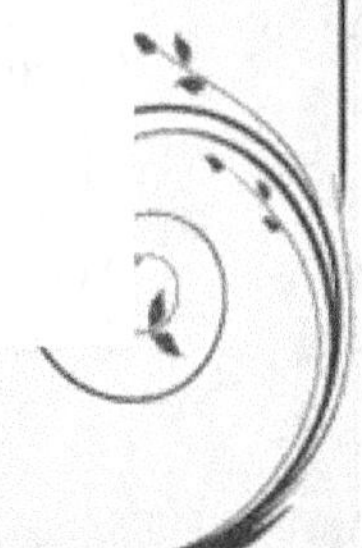

THE MEMORY TREE

The memory tree

In the barren abandoned

Deserted land of my very heart

There still stands this old memory tree

How old is it I know not

It just stays so unmoved untouched

By time and recklessly stands

This one memory tree my friends

Fate failed to uproot destiny said a damned prayer but

when some breeze passes on

A leaf just falls orange in autumn

Green in monsoon

Red in spring and yellow in summer

When it falls it reminds a lot

And there I go hiding the tears

No one could see smiles

At those moments relive it again

If it was for minuscule still

You made my life a meadow

Of colors that sang and music

That danced you took me in your arms

And made me a heaven of beautiful dreams

I lose my tiredness my lethargy my despair

And gain the might to fight the fate

Oh! The memory tree, a leaflet, and you

when stress and strain wears off days

when present and future seems drained

and confused the mercy of the divine

I think another leaflet falls from.

The tree...the memory tree

I reminisce the way I use to fall

On your chest, break in your arms

Cry out my pain and your lips on mine

Curbing it all passion with passion

The way I used to rest on your shoulders

The path and pressure I forget lost in your eyes to revive

again with double the strength

It fills my cup of soul with mirth

The life I lived Yes. Regret I not

it is all I have to bring a smile

that is like a lamp kindled in dark

the memory tree, its leaflets

it stands there in my heart ...as an art of

Kindness Life had no choice

but to leave.

WHAT ARE YOU TO ME

You are that gain in all my loss

The very passion in all my pain

You yes you...you are my hope in all my despair

You are that smile in my tears

You are the great revelation I yearned for

And you are my ultimate salvation

You are the wholeness in my imperfections

You the emoluments in all my transgressions

You are the sanity in my moments of insane fugues

You are the rain that bygone, my syllable seedlings of

verses

You are the sap of love that trickle from my

Wounds as anthems

You are the light that guzzles me the darkness

You are the sun ray's that kiss erase me the dewdrops

You are the winter fly and me the jasmine

You are the fire glow and me the firefly

You are the coziness of a blanket

that secures me in the cold bareness of reality

You are the breeze that flows through my wild hair

swiftly and softly whispering fear not

You are my awakening and enlightenment

You are all I seek and seek

You are the ocean you the mountain

You are death and resurrection

You are my soul mate peace

The indescribable peace.

You are me

the omnipotent God particle in me

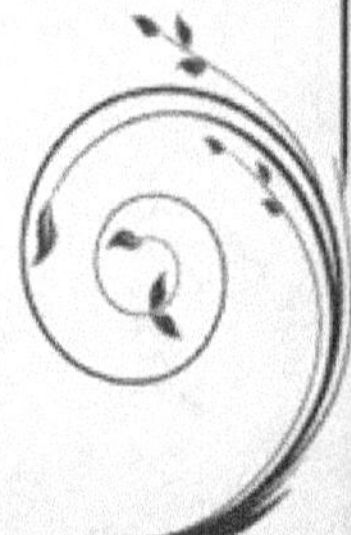

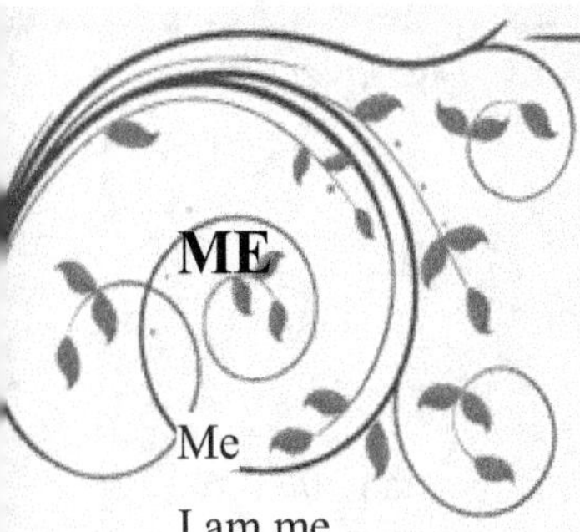

ME

Me

I am me

A woman a girl

She, the earth, the water, the fire, the flower, the breeze

the most ardent of everything

The creation and the creator

Yes the fragile me the most vulnerable me

The valleys of insatiable fragrance

from flowers of colors that lies deep within me and from

raising the peaks of frail love

Yet unmoved conscious power.

I embody the seasons and my emotions

My passions murmurs to you

The art of sustenance

I the -her

The woman

The left side of the journey, the path

The climber that flourishes on your table

The cradle that rocks your generation

You make me a queen in a day

You adore me in the temple of churches

In Dargahs

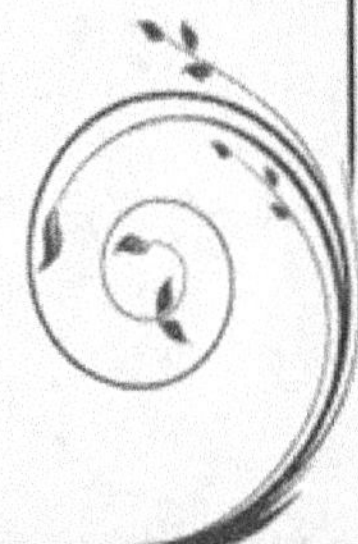

You adorn me with a veil and protects

In the Rob of sacred ownership call and its marriage in

exchange of my life-long servitude

You build red streets for me and makes me a commodity

and fix prices for my meat

reckless and ruthless society

Yes the very same me the Her

You make rules for Me

Every scripture has acts and regulations for me

Why me

The woman

Why am I only culpable

From six months to sixty years I am

raped racketeered rented relentlessly

When I raise

You call me a feminist

A reformist

That I hate men

No, I do love men

The protective hands, the understanding look

The caring hold .the compassionate hug

No one completes a woman than a man

A perfect man.

But again like ocean like rain

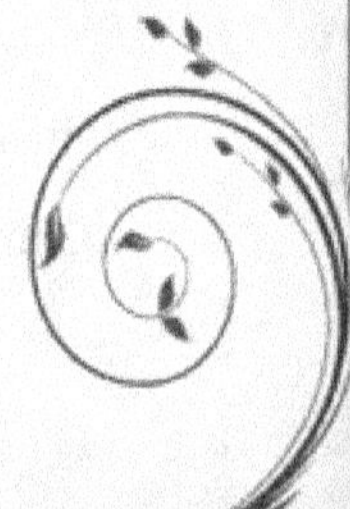

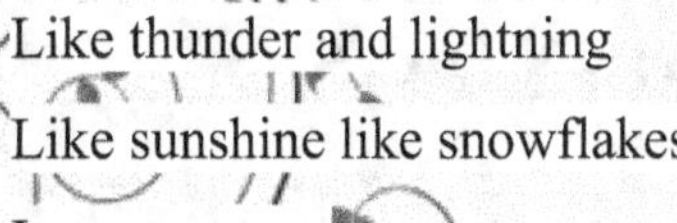

Like thunder and lightning

Like sunshine like snowflakes

I am a woman

The she

The her

The music and the dance

The love and the light

I am me the frail ....the strong ....me

I that manifested breaking the great silence

The great. She...all-pervading She.

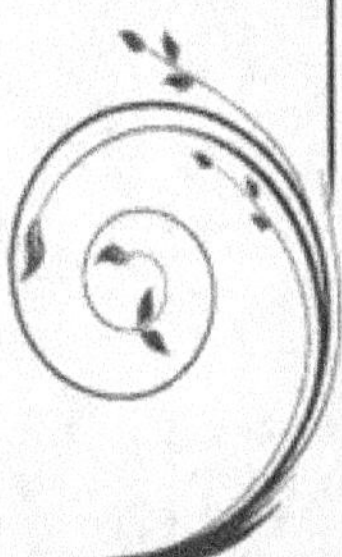

I MISS THE MONSOON DAYS

I miss the monsoon days

I miss the rattling sound

That raindrops maketh on

The roof tiles listening to which

My inner child calms down into a sweet slumber secure

like an earthling in vitro

I miss the heaving of tress like a virgin

In the arms of her lover swaying in the winds

The leaves that gently trembling quivering

In timid passion drenched in the raindrops

I do miss the fragrance of grass and soil

When water splashes on the thirsty mud

I fathom God as the wonderful artist

Creating the perfect symphony of everything

So beautiful so exquisite exuberant and exalted and still

never claiming any credits

When it rains so heavily my mind expanses

In to a transformation of peacock and I with my

beautiful feathers dances to the rhythm of rain

Where is the beginning and where is the end

I do not want to know I wish the till I quench

My voids enough all those raindrops

And then some seedlings would sprout in me
Of Eternal love which has no conditions
I miss the monsoon days.

I never carried an umbrella

I was a rain kid

A rain kid who believed

It purifies the soul

I miss monsoons a thousand hands of the sky by which it

hugs the earth

I made a paper boat ...

I just miss monsoons.

The sea the evening and monsoon and me and you.

A lot...of memoirs.

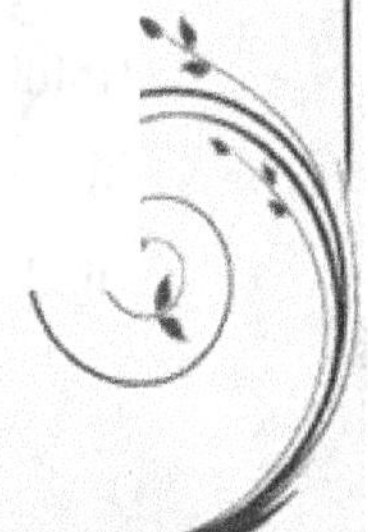

A BROKEN SITAR

Like a broken sitar

My heart vibes in the cosmic dias

And with anklets that lost their beads

I dance up to the notes in the roles

Pre scripted

Stop not your rhythms, the drums, the dolaks

The strings of your violin with divine vocals

Of the seven syllables of Raga

Let me forget the pain of a backstab

I do not want to let my soul weep on

There is nothing left of it

A deception, a treachery

A lifetime defamation

Still, I kept it in a corner

Wishing it never withered.

But when you just attacked

My friend to laugh at my pain

Brutally at this turn of life

I keep it going in my life

Holding it together

Just wondering

Of all the people my dear

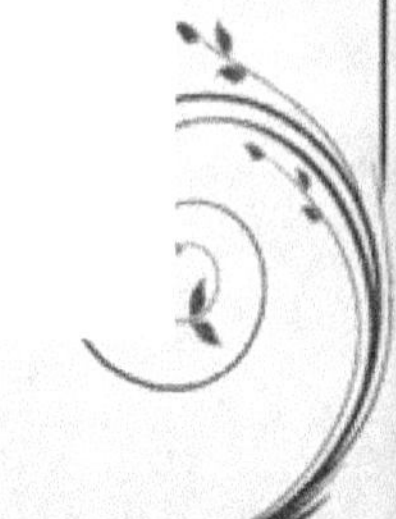

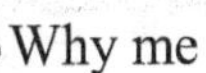

Why me

To carry the cross you need the purest lamb

For the ultimate sacrifice, you chose me.

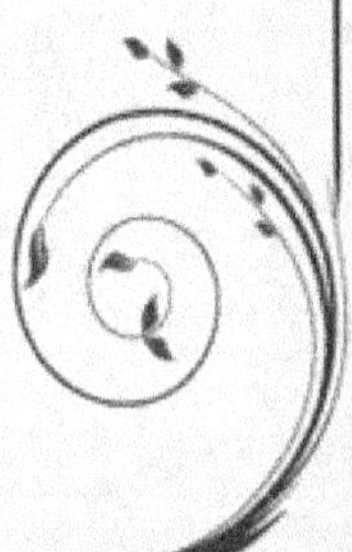

THE NRI INDIANS

For all NRI Indians caught up in rough situations trying

to go home

A nonresident

I am a nonresident

A rootless who just has roots

In hearts that bleed to seep into the land

Not to imbibe

Why do you fear me my land

My sweat and salt has drenched your veins

Built a new civilization

Wiped away a million hearts that wept

Those tears of mothers unfortunate

Sisters unmarried

Fathers who made nights a day

To fill empty stomach and souls

Now why do you fear me my land

There was a time when I would land down

People rejoice

Neighbors uncles and aunties

Which box to be carried which one to be opened

Which parcel is for whom

The day you saw me breathe in the air

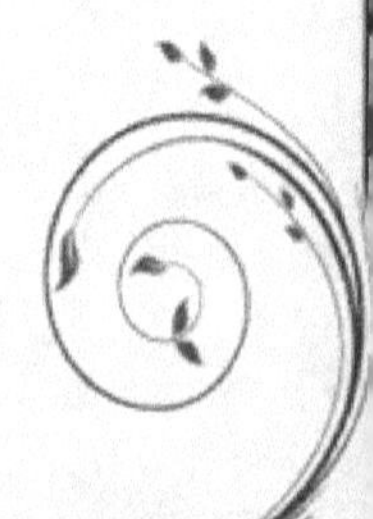

Of freedom, you asked me

When are you returning

I never annoyed any

Gifted all I had

I was celebrated

At my own cost

Did you ever know

What the desert and snow cause to man

Oh my land did you ever know my real story

I am a nonresident.

Do you ever know my moments spent in

Labour camps in lonely paths

In jobs that break your wish and will both

But when I send the money I earned

To enlighten your smiles

I feel I won the world

Now why do you fear me my land

Yes it is Covid

I know

But I am a resident

Who left my roots to enroot you

Why do you fear me my land

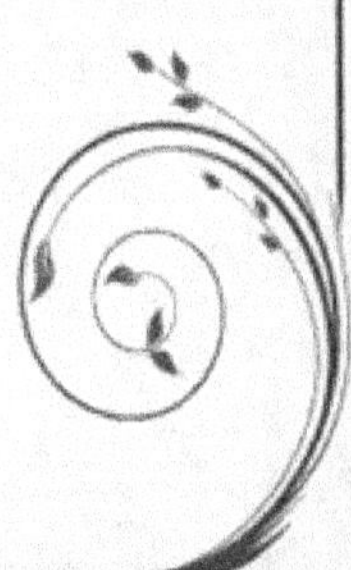

AT THE END OF CROSSROADS

At the end of the crossroads

When I took on the saddle

Dad, I am making it up to you

Fear I, not a bit anymore

Crumble fringe and fuss no more

For I am making it up to you

The slippers you wore

The miles you walked

And after those hefty schedules

The way you played both

Mom and dad

Little I know

It took me this far at least

The sleepless nights you sat

With me when I read the war of Panipat

I know when we grew up you taught kids

For a passion, I realize you were

Missing us but never could tell us

We were so grown up

At least I stiff-necked

In my tumult and torments

I never could tell you

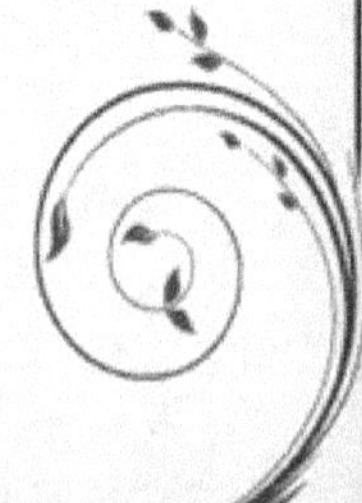

How beautiful were those days

When I held your finger and saw the world

How lonely am I now

Was I worthy of all that

The books you bought

Instead of gold

The promotions you canceled to care us

All I could give you was

My little girl and your time with her

But still, I never knew you were seeing me in her

When I turned to you

And saw the monsoon together

You lost the memory of half

When I bought you all I could

You lost its meaning full

I knew I build a little hospital room

Where you lay without knowing me

I still have not done your rituals dad

I won't I can't and I need you till I breathe.

But now when Life failed me

I fought it back with all my strength

I bounced back Dad I am your girl

Step by step one step at a time

I will win it back.

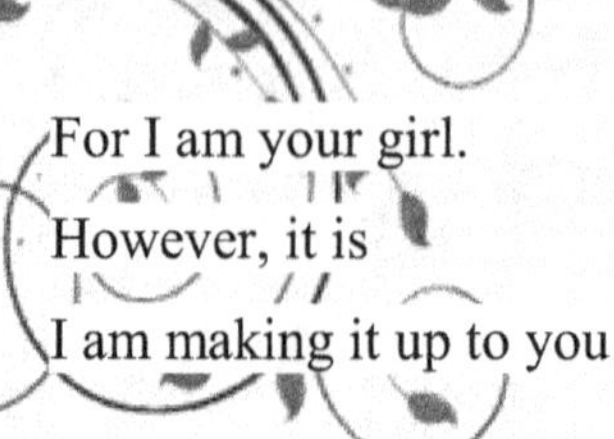

For I am your girl.
However, it is
I am making it up to you

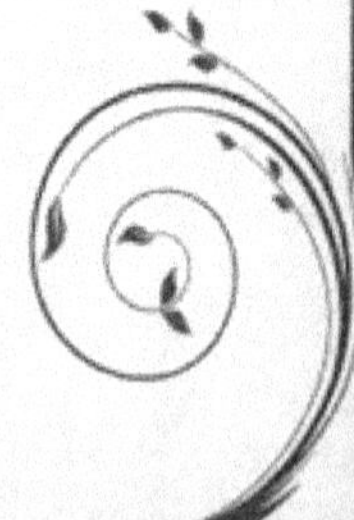

ON A LIE

On a lie,

Do not know why

Mind remembered you

Like a small station along the long journey of life's

railroad.

What do I compare you to

You were a lie

A lie that began in itself

Ended in itself

Some times on empty nights

I stare at the moon and think of you

Maybe you are a moon

That tantalized my innocence or naivety

But certainly, I am not your brightness any more I am

just the humble steady earth

That could only think

You were there, you are

You will be

But what has it to do with me

In the lanes of memory, I erased

You forever like a weed that

would never be replaced

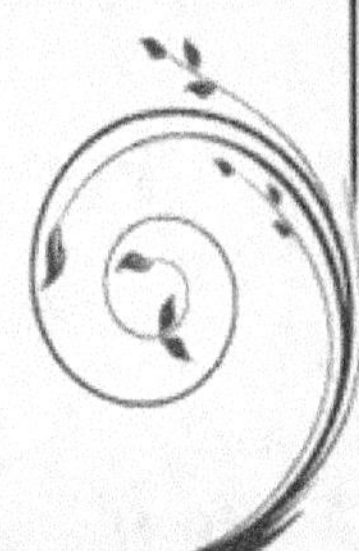

I know nothing hurts you much

You keep playing with hearts

Like a passion or game

Regret is not in your dictionary

I do not fret for you either

For you were a lie

A lie that cost me a lifetime

Still, I make sure when I rebuild myself

There isn't anything in your name

Not because I hate you

You don't deserve my hatred even.

But because you are a lie

A blasphemy that ransacks lives.

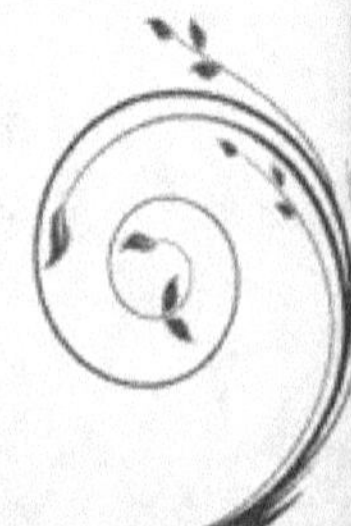

A DREAM

It is true my tripping mind dared to dream which budded

bright

Leaves around like a maze unclear

The wandering wayfarer in me only talked in a language

twisty topsy only another vagabond like me could

comprehend

This pilgrimage had a different way to breathe

A way to sing

A way to sleep and sit alone in endless nights in solitude

in fortitude.

It is true my friends

My tripping mind dared to cross oceans for this

unscathed dream

But being in this land It yearned for a vibe which was

congruent as mine blending into sonnets

On rainy and snowy days and nights

It danced to a rhythm to its own heart

Illuminating from within floating stardust over meadows

I just hold on to your hand

My nervous hand, happiest on to yours

For good or bad

My tripping mind

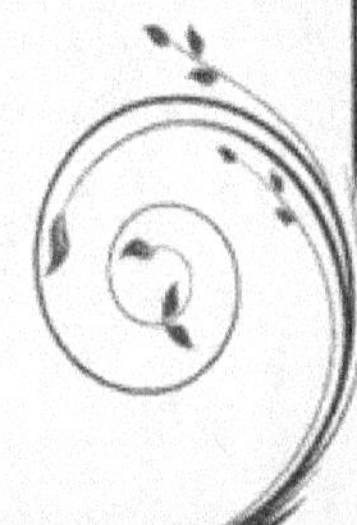

Oh my friends

Dared to remove the shady scarf of a veil

from my face inciting an upheaval of

emotions I struggle to conceal

My tripping mind

Oh my friends

Dared to dream

I am excused ... at the Altar of my conscience.

Just my conscience and that's all it matters.

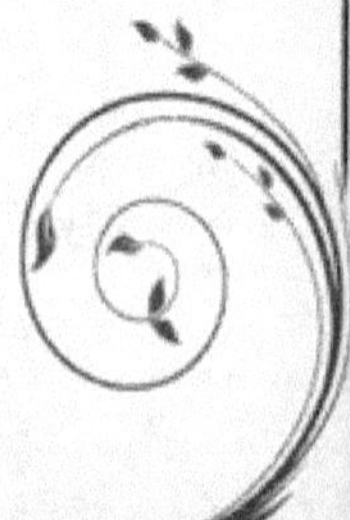

A BOOK

Life my friend

Is a book isn't it

A book of stories a book of poems

Good or bad my friend we don't remain

On the same page

We turn pages

Each page has memories

Good and bad

Stories of pain

Stories of hurt

Stories of passion

Faces my friend ..some ardent and close

To heart

Faces that that made us shattered in to

Pieces

Many unfinished tales untold mysteries

Moments captured of pious poise

Moments of abominable distress of nothing

Life is a book, my friend

We cannot be stuck on pages

On people we need to move on

Parents siblings children's spouse

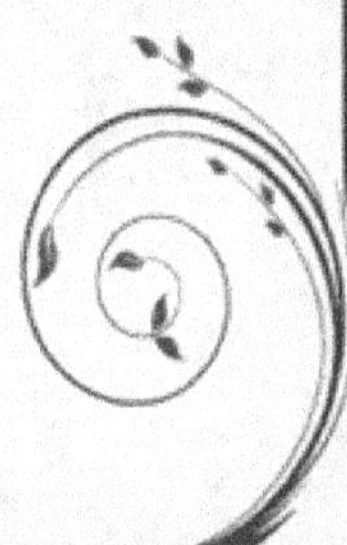

Lost love ..Crush...nothing stays

Turn the pages

In the end, before you end

You need to tell me what did you learn

From this rope walk...fire walk

Oh my friend

Of pains and gains

Of faces that haunt us like nightmares

What did they teach us

Of faces, we adored like godheads

Making us blush till the end

Dear friend

Of this book of life

It is just how you look at it

A tragedy

A divine comedy

A romantic saga

A thriller.

Whatever

of the stories ....complete, unfinished

the book is closed

Pages need to turn with wheels of time

Oh, my friend...

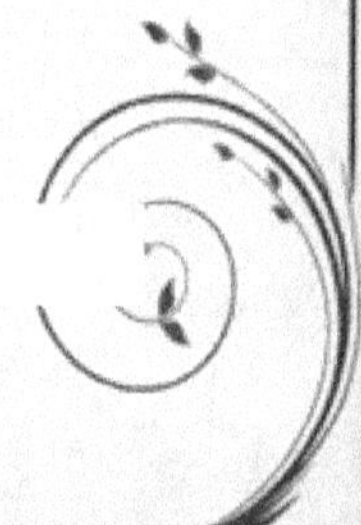

SHE WAS BEAUTIFUL BIRD

She was a beautiful bird

A bird who crossed oceans

To spread her love and light

She was in an exquisite garden

A dark and lost world and doom

And she came with a spring never seen before

Red blossoms green leaves Maple canopy

Such was those Virginian days

God ...none would forget

Heaven transcended on earth

She sang beautiful songs

Magical healing and her colorful

Feathers mesmerized bringing

Love harmony and peace

She bought life into the veins

Of even dead and decay

She was the holy note

Her fame spread wide

And there was a tired traveler

Who lived on the corner of that land

They met and the bird just fell it right

The ocean deep eyes

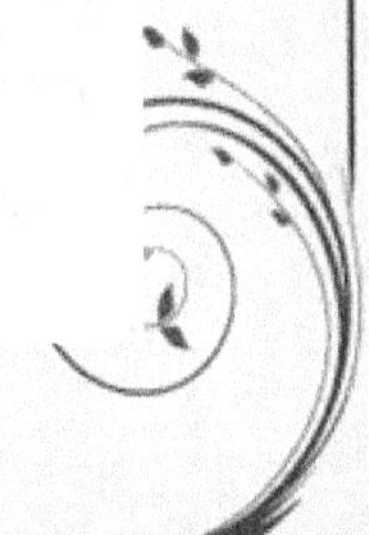

Her niche for a lifetime

Love was a bitter crime in those worlds

The Bird just lost the wings

It was cut so brutally

And she was thrown on the countryside

Days and months went

A good Samaritan soul

Picked her

Cured her

Today the bird just walk flies short heights

Striving heights building strengths

She sings for groups

She earns a living

She still makes her living hard.

The traveler found a lot of birds

He never bothered to turn

that's how this part of the world works

but there is a healer who is an alchemist

that keeps the bird intact...

He is not unworthy...not u faithful

That is how the east and west differs

East still goes by truth and love

West by lust and fakeness

Just as the traveler who was

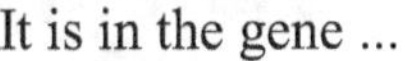

It is in the gene ...

The bird just goes forgiving smiling

As days go by

Spreading her love and light

With her broken wings shattered soul

Gathered to self.

You can't break her will.

You can't destroy love.

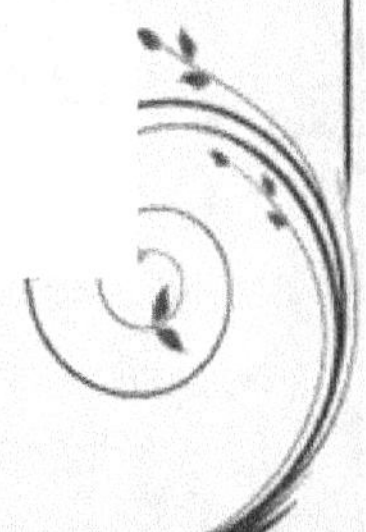

HEY!!!

Hey

Would you listen

Oh my friend

It is just fine to take it easy

You just gather yourself

Hold it together and if it must

Just break it down

It is fine to weep

Let all that out

It just not worth to stress out a lot

Because this life is just a matter of moments

Joined together woven and interwoven

Like the seasons

Like the colors

Like the day and night

One -ness and Duality

Blending and Diverging

Every soul you meet

Share their portion of love

Just their part of sun and

Their part of rain

There are walk-ins in life

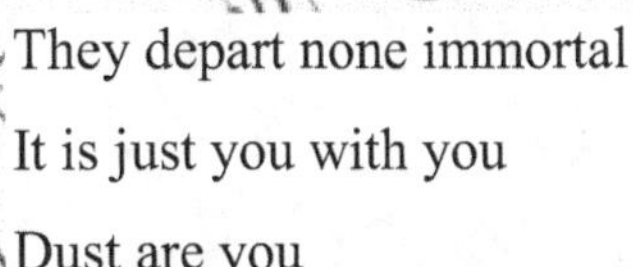

They depart none immortal

It is just you with you

Dust are you

Dust you become

What just remains is the memories

Why remain awake

When none bothers

There is a time to love

Then time to part

The business of this whole life

Is the celebration oh my friend

Of being alive ...just alive

Before you sip the next drink

Stop ..Don't do.it

just learn to live ...fall...

Rise...fall…rise again

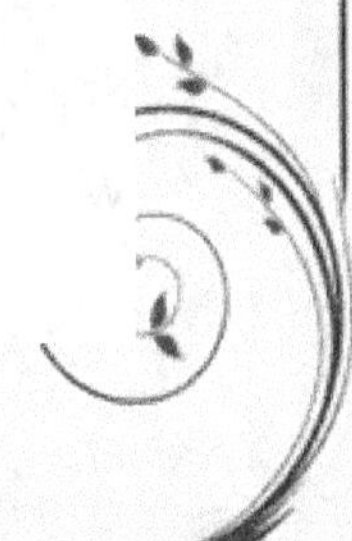

THE GIRL

I still see that girl

Smiling at me in my mirror

Through the tear-drenched eyes

I do see her in her words a girl

like poetry written from deep within

where colors dance and music is painted

That girl walking with her dreams

Lost in the abyss of love

With her light all around

Like sunshine and hurricane

Blended in one

Talking to herself amused

At times broken other times

Every time she lost

She got up with a strength

of thousand shooting stars

She was one of her kind

A girl who dares and cared

She swam against the stream

She battled with a tempest

When all that time offered was thorns

She gifted just flowers

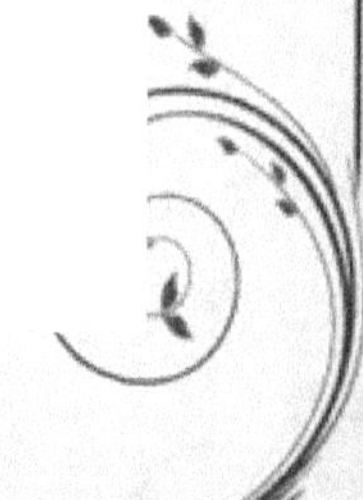

She was such a girl

A girl like a kite without its string

I see in the woman with anklets

With her adorning a passion

Of that girl .....

In my reflection, I see that

a girl who fell in love with the moon

Who walked her way like Meera

Singing and dancing in mirth

In pain in pressure in penance

I see a girl who won every heart

Like a breeze .....

Nothing can break her

nothing can erase her

she just sustains. A girl like a verse unwritten

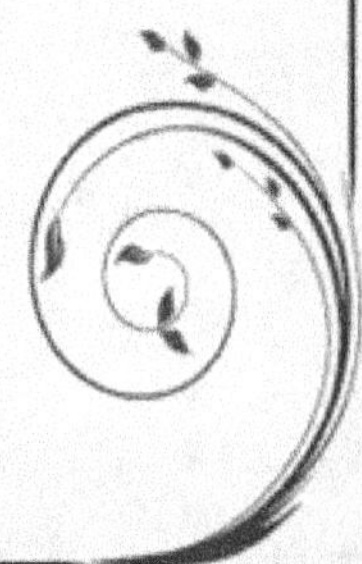

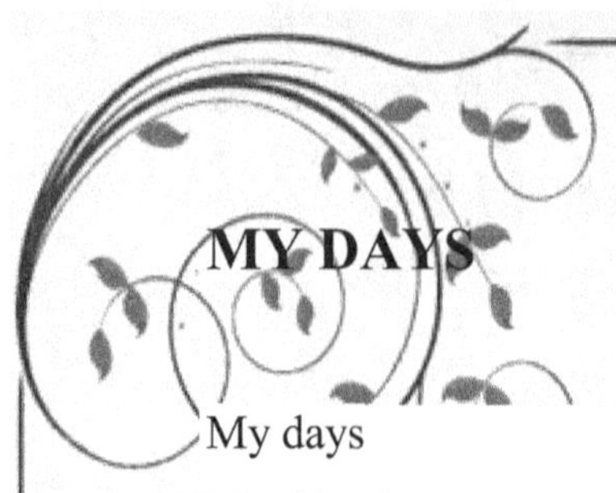

MY DAYS

My days

My friend

Is dissolving in absolute hassle

Buzzle of busy schedule

Which absolves in gratitude

Of my being and belonging

In a crowd, I lose myself and this persona

When the water runs on the soreness

I wish if it were your arms

Like the monsoon that embraces with

Thousand arms

My hair still falls over my shoulder

Like the climbers of snake forests

As you would describe

Black yet grey

Thick still untamed like me

Irresistible as you would want to say.

My eyes sparkling

Black grapes

With sort of tiredness around them

Yearning for your face

Midlife in the eve of these Dover days

I lose track of time and timelessness

Engulf me making the blossoms around

Seem paintings of a beautiful story

A story of me and you

A story of many people

I miss words in describing

An untold story is brewing in me

I feel light years apart

We still ardently love each other

In it lies my redemption

I revive from every death

I flourish and bloom

To be in the crowd

These days my friend

I do not see the moon at all

My sky is so aloof

I wish in your heart

There is still a portion of my little sky

Moon, sun, and land.

Just...like that!!

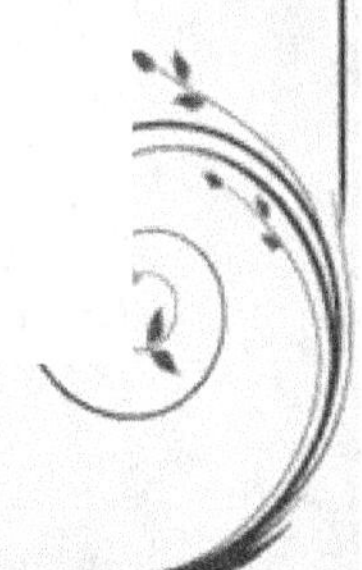

HER STORY

This was her story

She who lost a name

She who looked into the abyss

and told me smacking her lips

Red beautiful like mornings rose petals

A prostitute...among other slutty names

That's what he always called me

And legality liability laid upon her

Like a mark on her neck in a golden chain

Or the diamond ring

A lock can it be called so which patronizes

A human being to rule on another

A signature that becomes a seal

To make a being docile zip-locked

Lips tightened not to even let out

A cry .the flamboyant ceremony

Of cultural disaster that devastates

A woman ...marriage

Was she the only victim

No

It is a social virulence

Crippling a sector

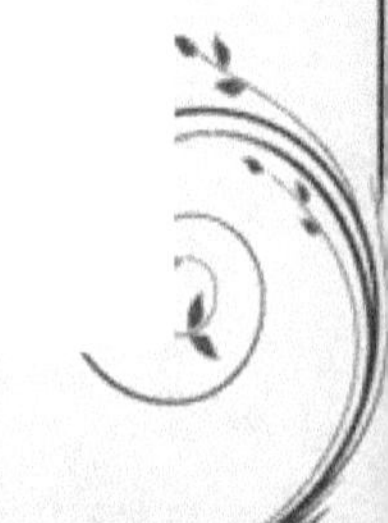

It affects all categories of all religions

It just exists and here I had her in front of me

The woman I happened to meet

Where why what and how

Is not pertinent but the reality

She was before me after her many numbers

Of suicidal failed attempts

Oh he kept her alive

Her torturer

She was a question mark to me

I belong to a country

Where Gold has to accumulated

The land has to spare

House to be made

And the girl to be a post-graduate

A car and the megalomaniac feasting to be prepared and

the traditional tempo to be

made in vernacular colors

For a girl child's parents

All for a custom and ritual of patriarchy

That is nothing worse than a sale at a meat market sorry

to utter

Domestic violence has no respect for geographical

boundaries

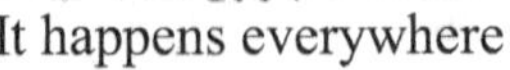

It happens everywhere

In a palace in developed and underdeveloped

It happens and when a woman loses her norm

She is an irony

She is outspoken

She is irreverent

She is not fine.

To be called a friend, a sister, a wife, a mother to nothing

...

Here Walked Many women

Who cared a damn

But men I am not against you

I saw in that married woman eye pain of years

Silenced suffering not finding a way

I saw in her strange gaze a plea to society

Your wife is another being

Not your punch bag to displace your

Rotten frustration

For a real man is a lion and a lion protects

The herd ...mean their pride

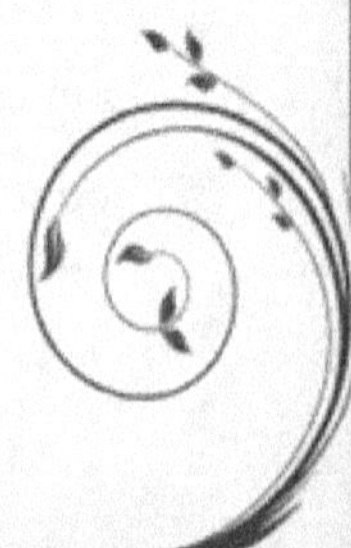

DAD MY COMRADE

Father, I can feel your heart

the laughter that always

masked a thousand pains

a single parent. ..who

Brought up two young kids

Giving up life youth career and fun

I do know it now

I still love the way you read the poems

The way you narrated plays and stories

Oh Dad when you taught kids for free

Little did I know you were missing

Us and you never told

You never read my verses

It hurt me a lot

But when my stepmom

Got my book with all compulsion

When you were no more

There to read on

I just asked her why in the world

And she retorted how do you know

He never read...you

Hey my friend, my comrade

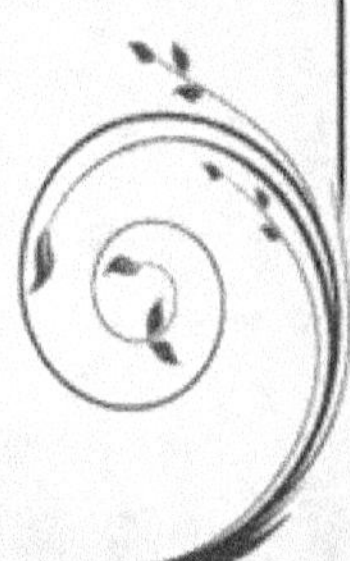

My guide philosopher

I never was your dream kid

Vagrant Vagabond...never made it up to you

Lost it somewhere

I don't travel anymore

There is no more a smiling face awaiting.

No more laughter

No more tears

Still, I raise a toast and make it up

Sir ...I don't give up

your little girl

is a fighter a better one Dad...

OF A LOST PAGE

Of a lost page

Why does that page remain

Still in the book of memoir

Not completed suppressed or repressed

Never sublimated nor even torn away

The remnants of a perfect illusionist

A pathological deceiver who vanished

From the lanes of memory

Just in front of eyes so casually

Apathetic An hedonic

With words well- crafted of an

Eternal coexistence

Evaporating into the abyss

Looking in search of new prey

The price paid for trust was too hard

To voice out

It took a lot to be back on my foot

Still, remember the innocence on that face

The saltiness in those tears

The way he just laid in my very lap kneeling like a kid

crying his heart out

I know among all the women in his life

That would be his liberation.

I expected nothing treachery was his way

It never bothered me

In my resurrection, I could just forgive him

As someone who just stamped my feet

Or poked my eyes unknowingly

Just....unintentionally...

I let it go ...

Oasis of plenitude is not with me

Deserts of solitude are mine yet

I detest yet think

what a master manipulator ...

What a mesmerizing innocence.

Oh lord

I still left that page incomplete

it had tears on it

mine and his

although parted forever

A CONVERSATION

The deep-sea once told the night on a new moon day

it has been a million years you gaze in mine and I in

your cataclysmic pitch-black depths.

All I need from you is be by my side and honor this

loneliness for just a few seconds

Tell me could you ever feel the pain

I hide with dignity in my laughter diligently

The catastrophe I hide in my tranquility

The gloom is in my ocean calamitous.

The night stayed silent, never answering.

The deep-sea pleaded in its sighs and broken words in

ruckle, the sea whispered in its quivers; don't you know

it?

When memories strike like thunderbolts

and random thoughts flash making

Silent ripples the pain in which I wrench in doom that is

unparalleled and I just wish to talk to you

my heart wants nothing but talk

the night seemed distant, cold, and apathetic

The sea said; all I had in me apart from salty dryness

was my words, my words that were

like sunshine spring and blossoms and whatnot, and
today, they just withered and forgotten, taken by the rift
of time

I am a shadow to myself and in such estrangement, I do

not even recognize me

To the hungry seagulls and lovers who lost

I am no solace any more

The night exchanged an empty glare

The deep-sea thus said to the dark night

I am nothing my friend but a heartbroken

Maidens drop of tear

Don't you see that

Don't you see me at all

Like a long lost forsaken flute

I sing for you...this song

Won't you listen to me the last time

These lonely moments are true somber

But don't you see life throbbing in it

The dark night did not give a damn care

The sea slept in a pool of anguish

Morning sun came

Waking her telling;

I have some golden rays

from the burning core inside me

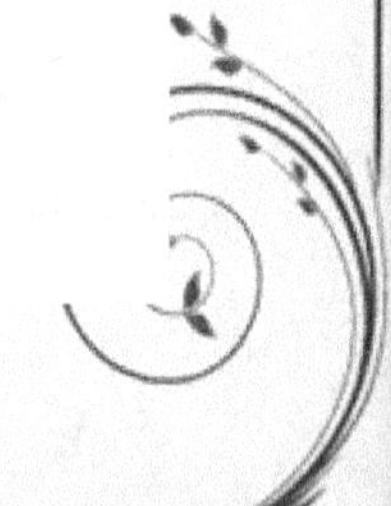

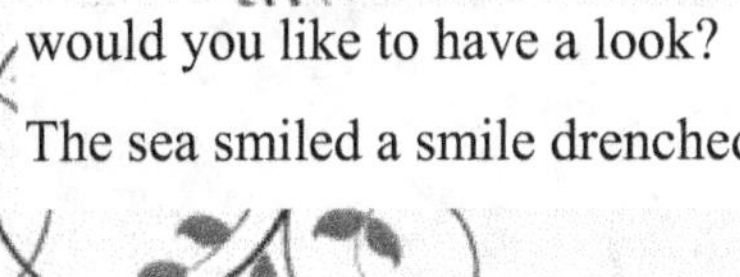

would you like to have a look?

The sea smiled a smile drenched in tears.

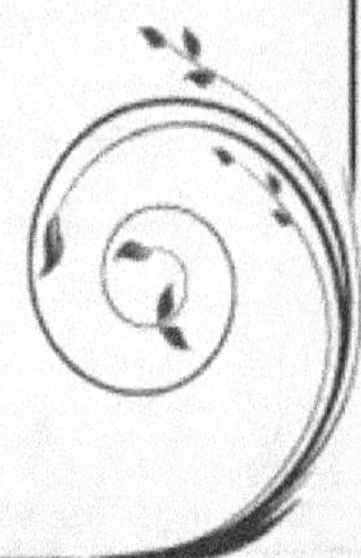

TEST OF TIME

In this test of time

God I look unto you

Straight into your eyes

With humility yes with humility

I am not Prometheus Lord

To leave my heart open

To be relished by Eagles of Zeus

For the sin of sharing fire of love

Which belonged to heaven

Nor am I Sita of Tretha yug

To be tested in fire and reconfirmed

My chastity my loyalty my credibility

The validity of my reliability

My sincerity my audacity

My tenacity my conformity

Are not going to be on trial

I know society demands to be stoned

Of the men spoken

Ram needs to look down upon

There are hands that unvarnished, unclothed

And laugh at your stark naked love

And naive innocence brutally by others

Call them any name from history

Greek-Roman Christian Muslim

None would spare a woman

But where I am against a man

I know there is a Krishna who would raise

When all else fails

I know there is a Jesus that held Marium

Against the whole world

I am not going to let you have another laugh

Insolent might over my kindness

My feminine divine is not a drop of tear

That you can tear it down

If love is my weakness then

In that very sacred offering to the cosmos

Let me blaze as a consecrated self

Absolving into nature

Let me be still in space less

Timeless spacelessness

Let me be one syllable

That is constant and pervasive

In that silence, I build my hermitage

It is ...time, the horizon echoed

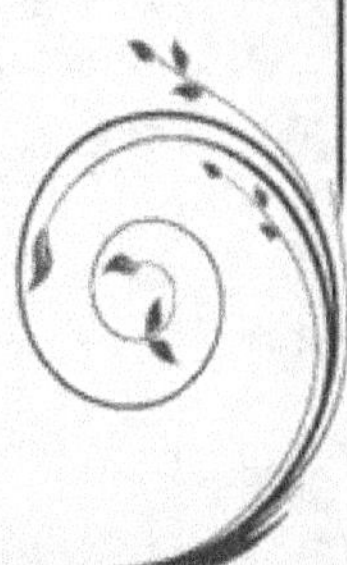

TO MY FRIEND

In the moments of applause and Belaud you showered of

my smile so infectious and innocent, never did I fathom

my friend my foe

you were trading my soul for tears and torment!!!!

In the moments of dreams, you painted on my

Canvases so exotic Spartan Nordic and exuberant with

colors so alive to be true never did I realize you were

erasing them from life forever. I dare not dream

in the moments of such days where I was healing

wounds. Being there for all I did care with my heart and

mind. You were inflicting the most painful wound in me.

It never did heal still bleeds.

In the moments I was trying to build you and your life

with light and hope. Pull you from despair to mirth you

made me an outcast forever snatching my name fame

and my purpose and existence. Made me a shadow from

the sunshine I was.

In the moments of these days, I don't but accuse you. I

silently walked away and nevertheless do exist. In my

portion of happiness and in my portion of satiety doing

things I can. Spreading light and love I still have. It is

hard my friend my foe to erase people like me who just stand for their own sake. Sorry to dismay you.

TODAY

Today

From my arms that quiver

Like maple tree leaves in

Autumn breeze, from my

Tight embrace that I have you in

My beloved ...don't walk away.

This day be still while You hear my heartbeats

Beating frantic and erratic but slowing

Down with your breath and its aroma

Making a symphony so ardent and enigmatic

I need to paint it red this day

This collage of our passion for making fusion and fission

of every minuscule of particles around, let us relish our

existence of being together.

Today

From my lips parted uttering your favorite verses my

beloved don't walk away

Because these are the only portions left

From the churning of cosmos for you and me

In the book of destiny where parting is inevitable, I need

to write this to the book of

Golden memories, which when I turn back

I need to quench my thirst from the eternal

Blending of innocence with beauty

And this alluring cross-section of life

I carved out from a book of life for just me and you

Unleash my love in me and in that bliss

Let me write the blooming of the wonderful lilies that

are rare and divine

Just this day ....don't walk away

Stay on till we make our freedom an expression of our

reality flowing in it

Forever ...forever

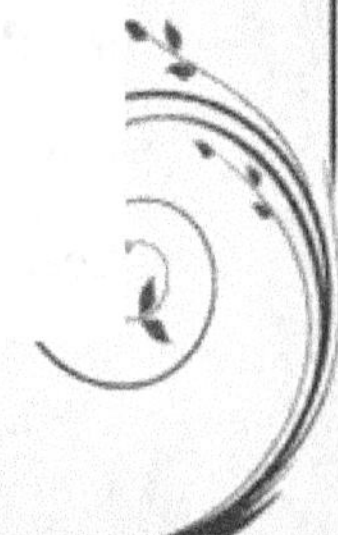

WE

When the moonlight strokes

My cheeks why do I feel

Your gentle long fingertips

When the star-studded sky enchants me

Bewildering me with your smile

Why do I become a sitar that reverberates

In melodies unheard heavenly

When these gentle breezes evoke

In a canopy of green trees a note

Leaving them to quiver I fancy

myself, lost in your arms

Resting my pain on your shoulders

Hiding my insecurities in your insecurities in your

Chest, my being dissolving in your ocean deep gaze that

churns my passion Bringing forth oysters with unique

Pearl's

When the sun Ray's softly open my eyes

I feel your lips against my forehead

Embalming my soul with layers of protection

In the world of thorns, your heart guards me

Day and night and like a rainbow

Leads me on and on

Strengthens me to meet another day

The raindrops remind your

Your chatter keeps me alive

Ignite the me, in me

You ...

My love like a peacock feather

Like a dewdrop

Like a rainbow

Like a melody

Are my fire and passion

And I am your light and way

We are one of two flexed into one

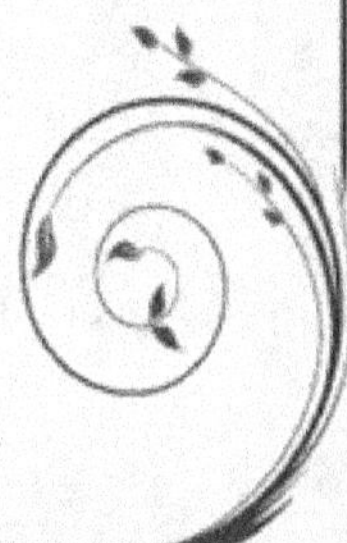

MY MIND

Oh my mind

Hear thou me

Fret thy not

These are not moments to fall

Brave thou are thine art be boldness

Uphold thy virtues values and faith

Your aim and goals may seem hard yet

Thy not quiver, steady be your gaze and soul

Thy journey be too lonely and smitten

Oh my mind

Hear thou me

Fret thy not

These days are not going to stay ever

These clouds are not going to cover thy sun

Thy smile is not wiped away forever

The dawn would come

Your hardship will bring success

The veil of darkness will lift

And you will walk into the light

There is no weapon against love

That you are

Nothing can break a pure will

As thine

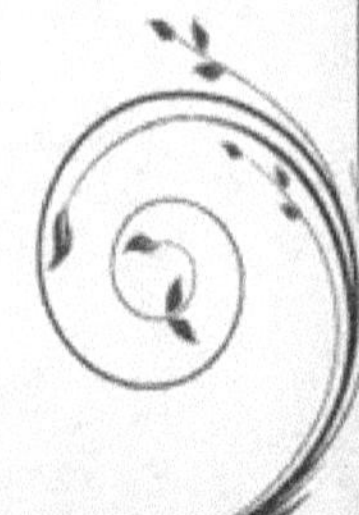

Oh my mind
Hear thou me

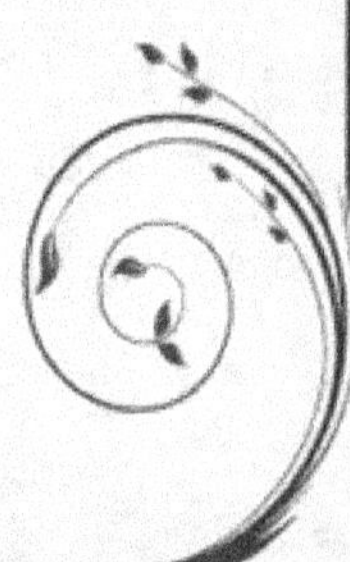

THE TIME

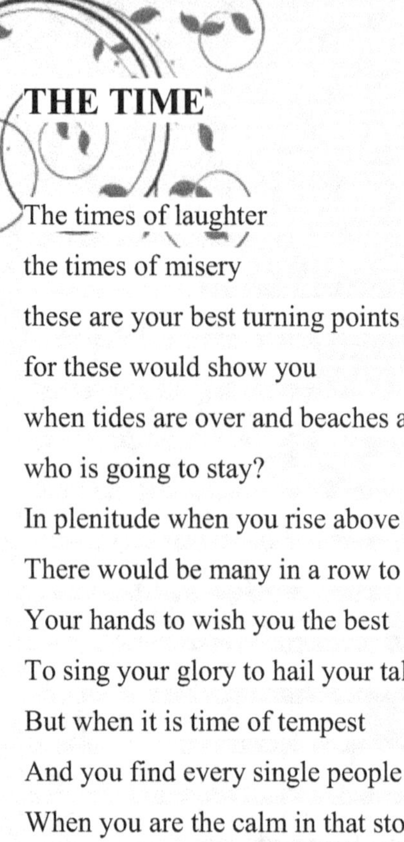

The times of laughter

the times of misery

these are your best turning points

for these would show you

when tides are over and beaches are empty

who is going to stay?

In plenitude when you rise above

There would be many in a row to hold

Your hands to wish you the best

To sing your glory to hail your tale

But when it is time of tempest

And you find every single people leaving

When you are the calm in that storm

You then realize some stay

Some ...true to the heart and soul

They aren't vultures that relish your flesh

Neither the crow that breed with greed

They are your people

Kith and kin

When shadows too fail

Frail are these moments

But ardent still to cherish

The times of laughter

The times of misery

They are the best teachers

They leave you with lessons.

Never to forget that

that love everyone for

there is innate good in all being

but your trust...oh never on man

Just on your higher self

Lord or God ...however you call.

ONCE

Once

I want you to feel

Me beneath the mask

Caressing gently on those wrinkles honoring

Them in silence which can converse

Among us

In the valley of memories

Mind gets lost in unbounded pastures

Under the dusk of saffron sky

Where the sea swells in tides

I like to rest my head on your

Shoulders and look beyond

Once

I want to breathe the fragrance

Of sandalwood in your sweat

So strange soothing me

Blending with air so divine

Holding me together

Whenever I fall apart

Strong stronger as ever

To fight another day

Every day

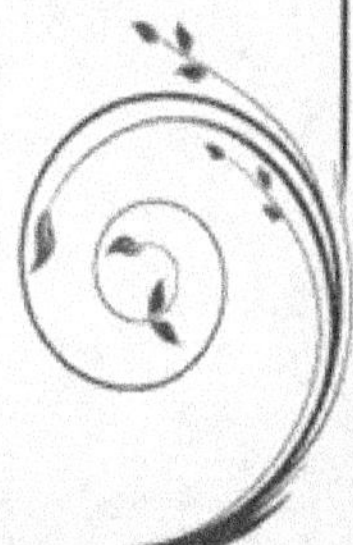

Once
In these days
Where life has a different
Meaning which I do not
Want to comprehend
And yet know deep within
I learned to think
There is no more
You or me
We are one entity
Beyond time place and destiny
I write us to eternity
Once
I wanted to wrap myself
With you and moonlight
When the sitars are played
When the songs won't end
When the anklets never would stop
In that shores of peace ....
Once

MY LOVE -MY EMANCIPATION

From the heights of

Consciousness glittering in deep

Contemplation you sprout

My love as perennial spring

of enlightened flow

Drenching every spiral note in me

Awakening the ancient in me

Like holy drops emanating from

Cosmic conchs of complete dissolution

In the specks of spells of these moments

You fill in me like the bliss of awareness of light

From the shores of dreams unknown

Where I lost my self in totality

You transcend me into a new reality

Reminiscing and renewing

I find myself at peace

In the thousand petal lotus

In this, I find my emancipation

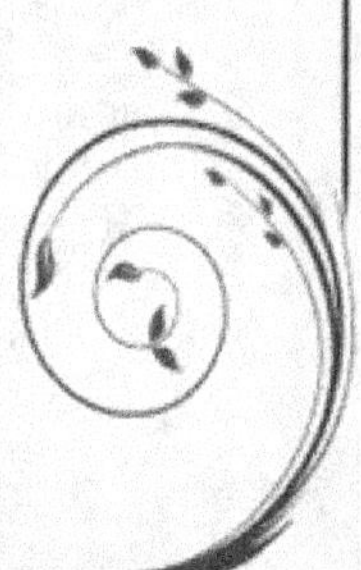

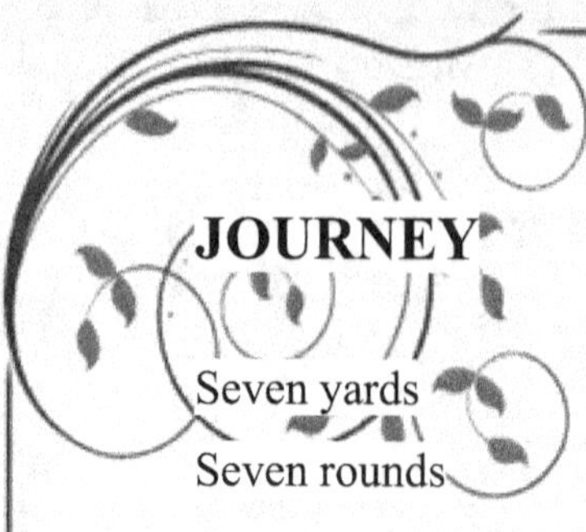

JOURNEY

Seven yards

Seven rounds

Seven vows

Our journey began

The fire was inside me

The fire was inside you

We burnt to be our light

It is a journey in a storm

It never was but our hands never

Left apart

It rained and snowed

And in the scorching heat of deserts

We tarried not falling apart

Whatever destiny gave

We turned it in our love

To light and bliss

And shared our pain and pleasure

This journey my friend

Until eternity

Nothing to give

Nothing to take

Knowing the soul from within

Forgetting the erring

Forgiving the shortcomings

We stood the test of time

Being the armor of one

Another being the peace

And war, making a lifetime

Seem so unique

This journey oh my soul mate

No guilt

No fear

Nothing obscure

Plain simple serene and sanctified

We have come a long way .....

Seven yards seven rounds seven vows

The fire in me, the fire in you

Till pyre...this journey oh my friend

Birth rebirths of this togetherness

I carve it out from the wheel of time

To timelessness forever...

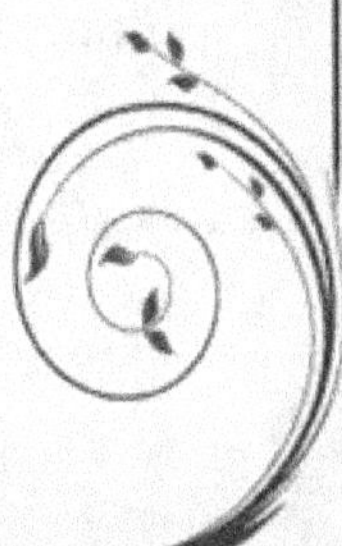

THE ENCHANTRESS

No matter what the world said

An enchantress

An enigma

A river that damn care shores

A drama queen

A poet a poem an art in itself delight

A witchy witch

A jigsaw puzzle to solve

Underneath the mask of a smile

A story is written in gloom

A fire to yonder

A firefly to yearn

A hurricane not yet tamed

So to the sailor, they asked

What is she...

He would laugh at it

Laughter that reminds him

But in his arms, she lay

Like a child who thought

She won the world

The eyes that told

Many stories

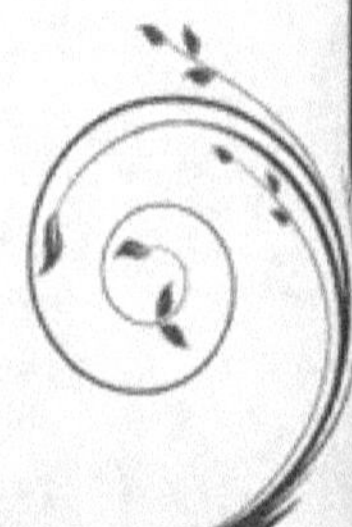

Mesmerizing luring conquering

The look that peers into the souls

Drawings colors that just touch depths

In his arms, those eyes just twinkled

Like diamonds stars like all that glittered

He did not want to disturb the petals

A flower- she was there in his arms.

Benevolent beyond human

Every night in his sleep that innocence

Bloomed like a celestial being

It spread through him

Took his sleep and made him

Say a prayer in her name

No matter what the world would say

He just told the world She is...oh dears

The bliss of nature. Serene divine

A rain that showered and passed

A breeze that whispered and vanished

But he never told the world he made

Her into a pearl, sew into his core

And there is no more of her left.....

No one heard of her

No one saw her

The Enchantress as they called her

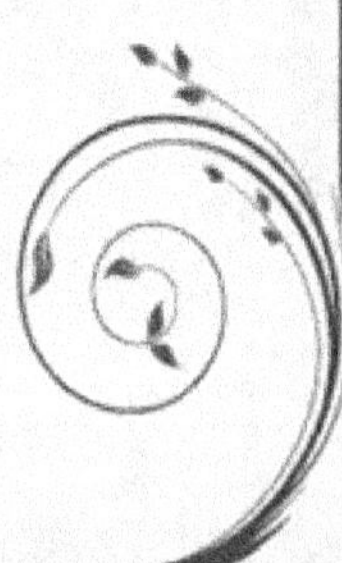

MY HAPPY SONG

Are you my happy song

The song that ancients sang

In the wilderness

Every beautiful pregnant mother

As in dense African tropical deep woods

Would sing to the tree of life

The tree that belongs to her

The tree of destiny

Which lost meaning in the modern world

And each day the baby grew

Hearing the mom sing it to the tree

It binds the matter to life

It binds the roots to roots

When she was in labor

The elder women sang it

The baby grew up with it

Whenever the world went wrong

The song kept the child go on

Thus it was .the happy song

It healed broken hearts

It patched wounded souls

It just made the hearts in symphony with the divine, the

water, air, ether, fire, and earth

Should I call it a mantra

Should I transcend realms

In peace and bliss with it

Are you my happy song

Are you my primordial bliss

The tree, the African women

The monk's ink .....

In one-syllable; me, you, and the cosmos

churn into one ...

The one with eternal peace

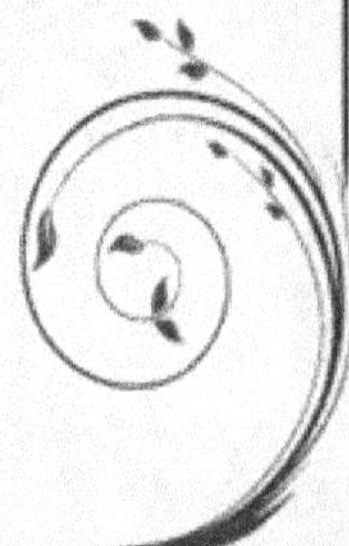

TIRED AS A HELL ...

Still, I smiled to self

Dad is it still your way

To gulp it down, take it lightly

Just do it and don't ever complain

Because life is never a bed of Rose's

There are a lot of others

Who just fight their battle

In ways which your fussy girl

Cannot fathom

So I just learned to say

I am thankful for every speck

Of these moments

I felt you with me

When I tarry and tread along

To give up and crumble down

Was easy but I learned to

Get up and go on

For you still would say

Oh come on girl

Do what you got to do

And leave the rest to Lord

Life is till the breath goes on

It is written in colors

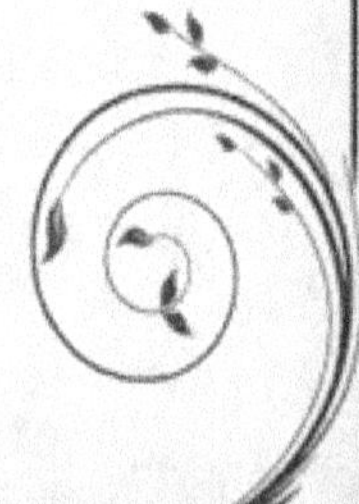

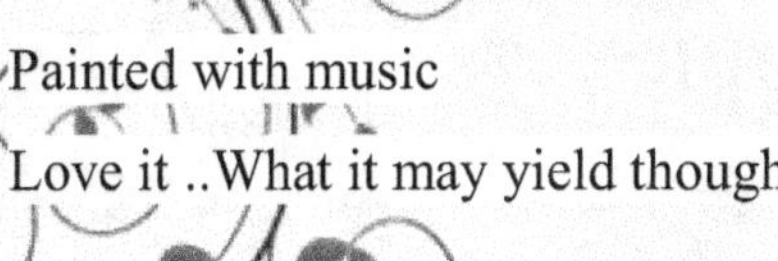

Painted with music

Love it ..What it may yield though

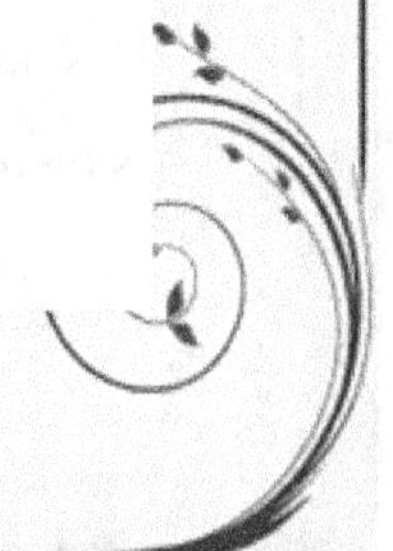

A SONG FOR SOUL

Is there a song

That could be sung for the world

The people who are front-liners

Everywhere in every walk of life

Bowing the heads

Deep in the silence of our hearts

With a love that we could just sing

That would brighten up their days

The Mark's on their masked faces

Their smile and selflessness

For all of such beautiful souls

Is there a song

If it is dark

We can burn and be light

This pandemic has not won

We have won many like before

A song for soldiers

A song for our lost ones

World for all that

Has done until this just let it go

Is there a song for tomorrow

That is yet to be blown

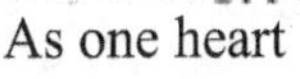

As one heart

One soul one mind

Oneness in whole

Is there a song

For those who battle life

Shoulder to shoulder

To save lives

At their cost

Then let us just sing it

Song of true wellness peace prayer

And harmony forever in this world

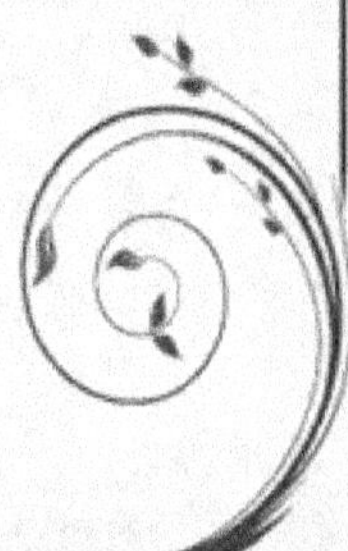

BROKEN KITE

I told you I am a broken kite

String less just about to

Vanish in the abyss

Flying free in that bliss

I never want to bound

Patched repatched and flown

Perish is contentment

To that flamboyant preciousness

You just told

I am not the canopy of trees

Dude, I am the Sky

The space cosmos

Feel free to fly in my love

What do I tell you.

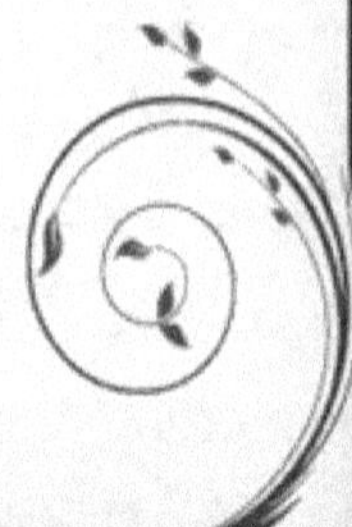

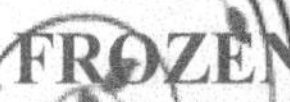

FROZEN

Words unspoken unspeakable

Tries to find their wings in shattered mutilated soul

trying to find adorn a frantic smile worthless, little can

be faked

Wounds healed throbs with unknown hurt

Tears....don't flow down

Frozen is my heart

Ice cold my thoughts

Underneath your vast sky

I knelt before you Lord glaring

Into your deep eyes pairing my

Pain and passion with yours

I recede in my silence with

Reflections and find frozen

Alone aloof on my path

I tarry holding my brokenness together.

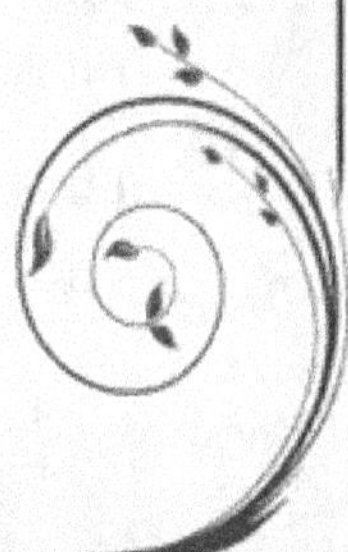

I REMAIN

Like a tree when the autumn

Leaves shed in fall

Like the sky when its stars

Burns down and fade

Like an oyster that is broke open

And the pearl took off

Like the shore that witness

Tides rise and recede

Like a lamp whose

Wick is burnt over

I remain

Never bothered of the

Names attributed

Defamed Derogated

Like a love that is not conditional

Like an old city abandoned

With no glory yet surviving

I remain

Like the dewdrops like the rain

Like the breeze in dry deserts

Like a poem, like a promise

Like a prayer like a truth

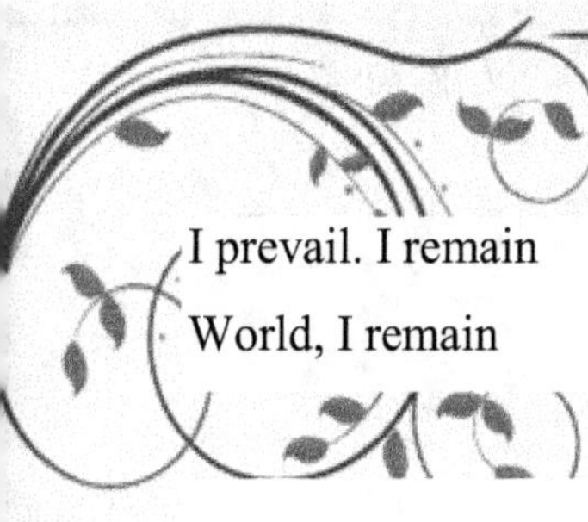

I prevail. I remain

World, I remain

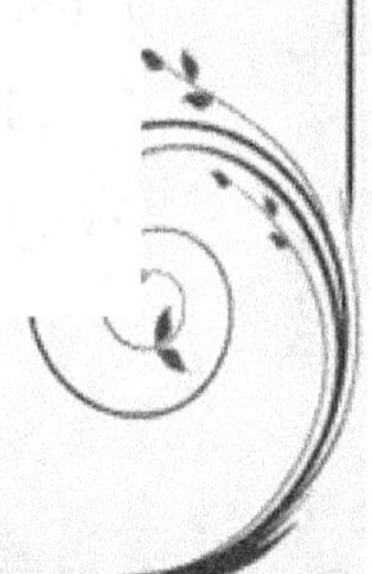

DEAR VULTURES

In and around my life you relished

As carcasses of a century

With your reputed moral beaks and claws

Which you have torn up to see through

Enough up to your unquenchable social and ethical

satiety and pseudo norms

I would say ...there is nothing new

If I have served the purpose of becoming

Spice to your evening tea discussions

And small talks and your favorite night gossips just

leave me alone

I am existing with the humility of a feather

You can never measure or comprehend

I survive on the hard-earned bread of my sweat and I

am not asking your companionship nor your hatred

The choices I made, the roads I took

The cross I carry, I tarry alone.

I bleed alone I weep alone

I fight against my fate alone

Yes, I do suffer from sickness

Yes, I stumble from deep trauma

That binds and slay but I strive a bit

Every single day to excel to grow beyond

Its clutches that makes me fit to stand another day to

live for those who still trust in me

I may not have celebrated narrations

But yes a small world to protect.

So before you make soap operas on my life

And spread it like wildfire I pray to you

Just leave me alone

It is done ...you are pounding on carcasses

And there is nothing new

Just half-healed unhealed wounds

Don't poke it open

For heaven s sake

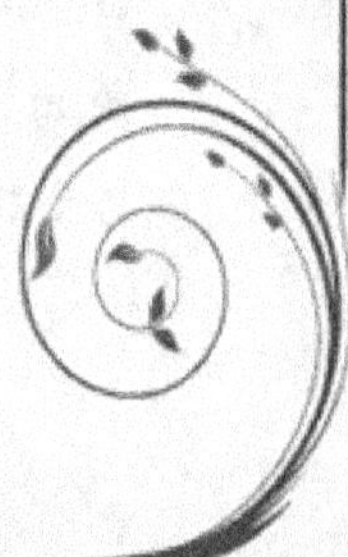

TO MY CREATOR

When you mold me

Cement me and fill me again with the molten piece of

gold right into my heart piercing where it hurts most

...oh my magnificent maker, the omnipotent artist

Like the Japanese vase, I stay

Beautiful with poise and humility

Broken and not worried about it.

Finding your utmost love in every minuscule

Of moments.

If it was to end happily ever after

Wouldn't it be there those tales

Those poignant paths those people

Those pages monuments and great mansions

Tears have drenched very many

Creations

Art in the heart has pain

Lives waged at the cost of fear

Was or is not a choice for many

Destiny by itself is a path

Straight-line don't manifest

And the more you try to unfasten

The more ties strengthen leaving

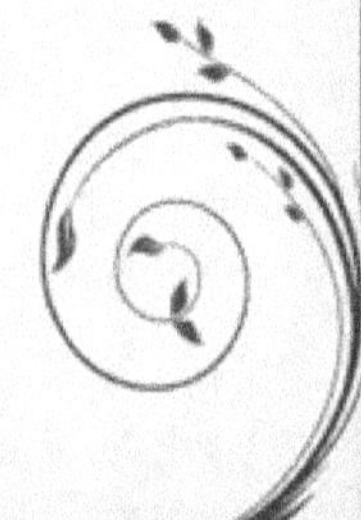

Scars of abandoned battles lost

But for a noble cause.

Yesterdays have worn out torn blanket

Of cozy memories!!!

Would it shield from thoughts

That shudders marrow with shivers

And pounds as thunderbolts in mind

In this brittleness, there is immense power

In this despondency, there is the will to hold on

Love never fails nor gives up

It blooms as the innocence of a flower

Like a star fell...but glowing to enlighten

To kindle, my heavenly sculptor

Like a Japanese Vase with gold

I am trying to find my perfection

Amidst the imperfections

Being beautiful like a verse...

Withered deep divine decoded

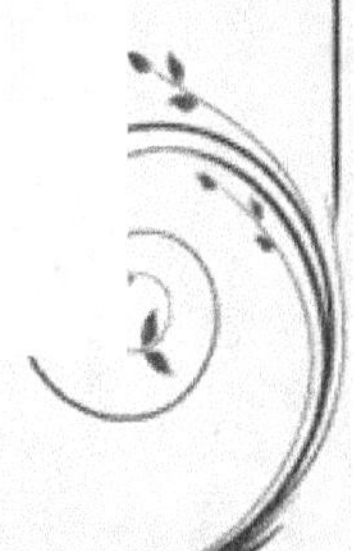

LORD

Like a wick of a single candle

Lighted in a lone altar

In the storm in the rain

My eyes seek you, Lord

If all it needs is a prayer of a true heart

You have it all but don't forsake

Like a single stanza of a psalm

From the deep pain from the due faith

As the red sea as in den of lions

If all it matters is the trust of

A pure and soul of your lamb

You have it all but don't forsake

Lord between us there is nothing

You can see me through

As Jacob's Lord Daniel's God

As did Job and David's Lord you

Could move the mountains

Then my Lord

If blind did see and deaf could hear

I ask of thee ...Lord shower your blessing.

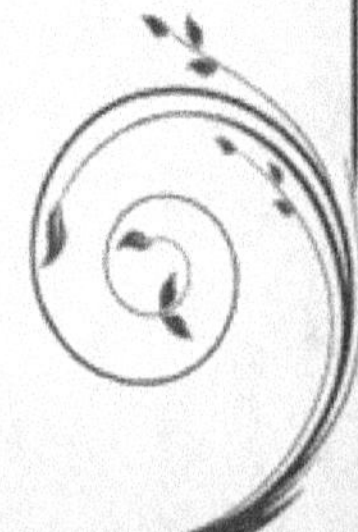

SPEAKING OF LOVE

It is never incomplete

It is just finite and self immersed itself as

A gentle ripple reverberated in the universal mesh it goes

in perfect circles and cycles.

So me being portrayed as a lost soul

Does not add up

I am the same ceaseless flow of pure

And inexhaustible love that never expects

It is my truth my blessing my curse

My tragedy and my greatest success

My weakness and my greatest strength

In this journey of valleys and steep peaks

Of swamps, marshlands mirages, and seas

People meet they remain and walk away

Seeking their purpose

If ever the roads crossed and in a

Parallel reality you exist

Let the prayers of green rosary beads

Guard your paths

I bind myself with that ardent memory speck.

I am, complete in myself

There is nothing or no one that love could seek

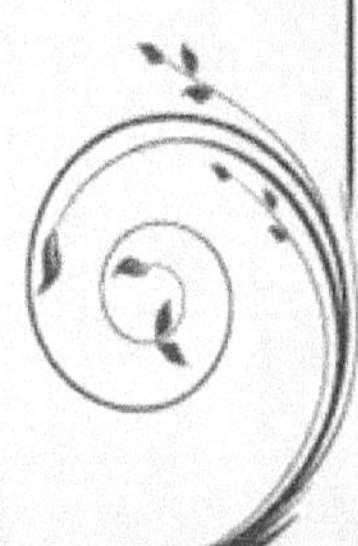

My love is whole in itself

Let it be your star at West

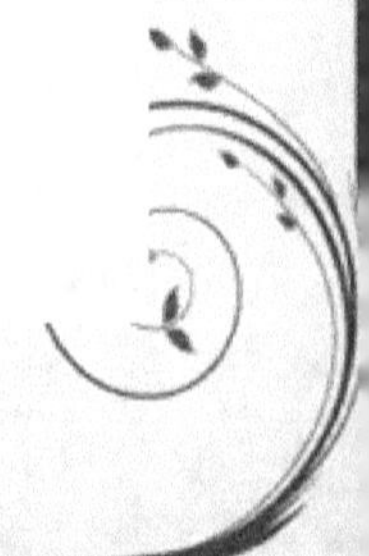

IT WAS A JOURNEY

Short

Me and you

Started inevitable

Every journey is not itself a complete one

It was just like the autumn leaves

We cuddled and parted

Leaving hurricanes in the heart

That uproots trees of existence

Every time our paths crosses

Our thoughts get entangled

It shook our grounds leaving

us drenched in passion and pain

But it was destined you take a turn and never return and

it was someone else to hold your

Arms thick and tight

Parted are some love enchanting

Which finds meaning in a prayer said

With purity and utmost serene intentions.

To guard the ways

For to forgive and take the blame world painted on

and to experience it every moment needs a true heart.

And when it blesses you are taken care of

CALM IN MY STORM

When the world was inside me

You waited and watched

When the world did blackout

And I felt flesh and a par

I saw your silhouette seeking me

In most places where none could reach

If it wasn't for you

To be the calm in my storm

I would not have made it a bit

Live from dead and decay

When I held my arm out at you

Pining with my entire being

Burning in my own tribulations

Wrenching at what I could not hold any more

You heard it all and took into your wounds

Our cracks crevices bleed absolving

Into the freedom of a feather that

Fell apart at your feet

If it wasn't for you

To break with me taking lashes

Turning to ashes those blasphemy

I would not have stood the fingers

That raised against ruthless on my soul

When I wept tears hidden out

That borne shadowless streaks

That none heard bothered

But broke me to core and

With your words, you could wipe

Away from it all in a split of seconds true

When the world just darkened when it all blurred

You came in gently...

You kindled Hope's lost and perished

With your love that is precious

You proved me worthy

You proved me true

In all my perils at the end of all discord

You remain and I am not alone

It is just this time the fruit is ripe

A master knows the season.

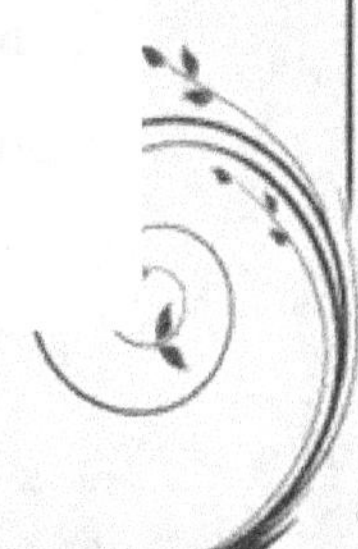

IN MY SILENCE

In my silence

There are a hundred thousand words that speak only

of

Calmness truth and harmony

If ever your heart seeks it

It is written on the blue clouds of despondency with

Silver laces of hope and trust

In my tears

There are a million smiles hidden that

Kindles every lamp those are blown

With a love that judges not and yearn back not

If ever darkness fills in your soul

You can just find light in the cross

Right where you bow in the altar

In my coldness

There is a passion burnt and buried

Yet so alive pervading the trivialities

Shining like sun deep in every drop

Of self-given to the good of the world

If ever you feel that you are failing

Look through the maze you can see

My shattered wings yet keeping in the plight

Never giving up.

Every pain

Every fall

Every valley, every thorn, and stones

It is easy to keep hiking

If it was taken for the cause of love

In me

You can see the sky and earth

For I exist as they exist...

THAT AUTUMN

I still thank the autumn

Leaves of the Maples canopies

And cherry blossoms

For your friendship

When it all fails and I succumb

I still feel your smile and coffee

The aroma that fills in when

When the head is held high and

I smile at new faces good or bad

I keep the battle going on

Your German Gene's or stoic trait

Or your life at crossroads

That you just tried on

Never bothered, unshaken

Like a breeze my storm

My hurricane my thunderbolt

Friend, a woman of honor

Beautiful and bold, mother

A sister-friend whatnot

Guide philosopher and the way

A road less traveled

When orange leaves

Fall off laying amber beds

In pathways in my Dover life

I write this day to you

I know you read my throbs

Through, unmasked be me

In the rare words we share

I am me staying by the truth

I could not be someone else

I see the October skies and sigh

What an October it was that seized

My world in a split of seconds...

My people all that I cared for

But you ...you are my gain

A gift that doesn't change with seasons.

A friend....that is meant to be.

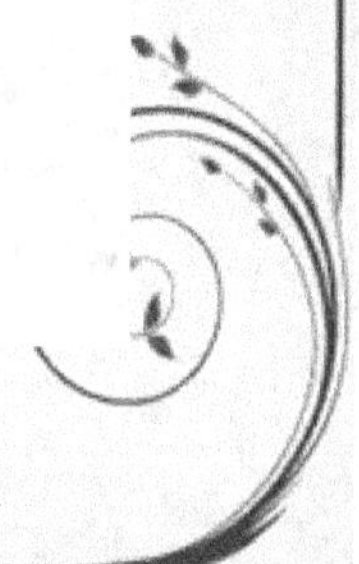

THIS JOURNEY

Am I the traveler or the means

But the rest of all are just

Stations or stops

It has never been like this or

Was it always like this

I am the witness and life

Goes on

On this stage of the cosmos

How many versatile roles

The play never ends

Each time a different costume

A different dialogue a different makeover

Faces come and faces drift

Travelers none stays forever

To hold on to own to cherish

Is holding the water in palms

Change is the law that prevails

And pervades every matter

Every minute to live it fully

To transcend beyond the worries

That unforeseen tomorrow holds

When you don't have a second in-store

Mind over material and soul over mind

The soul being a part of the whole

Resonating in the primordial peace

Seeker and seeking becomes the same and there is

nothing but a stillness

In that stillness, I unwind the cocoon

Of pain and impressions of pathways

I decode my codes and set them into a

Fire winged species of a bird...

That has nested in the burning sun.

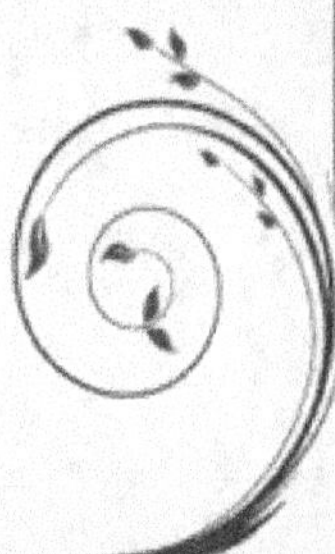

SERENDIPITY

Of this very life is never

My fury and never I detested

A speck of it nor have I

Not lived it whole in fruition

But I think aloud

Are pain and pleasure given in equity

Given or taken

We are the slaves of our choices

Some, at least or say me

For many think better

Who levies taxes on our deeds

Is karma every body's friend and guide

Like a credit card my happiness at times

Scared me, for I started paying it with

My tears and like any rented outfit

And the Apartment I tend to keep my

Debits and credits balanced.

Though memories haunt my existence

Like bills that have to be addressed

I keep a check on them and run rat races

In its harrowing ruthless truth

Me ...on this earth is in this very body is

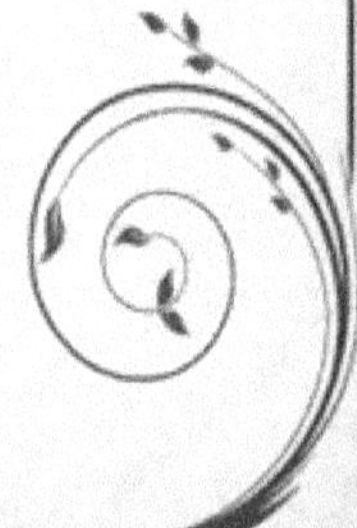

a circle, point completeness.
To stay in the moment
I realized there is no amount
Of training or coaching needed.
When you just value moments
You master the very art of living
Past present and future all
Just illusions of time and
When one understands the magnanimity
Of time... would time spare him
For a narrative
When senses can no longer
Tickle the mind and nothing
Perplexes you death or birth
And that mind is under your
Control you make a lot of sense
Between a breath is held and out
I awake to sustain and absolve
With the innocence of a flower
After the most beautiful monsoon
I look at your life, in your eyes
Serendipity of this life
As a wonder, the kid was and is
A surprise that mesmerizes

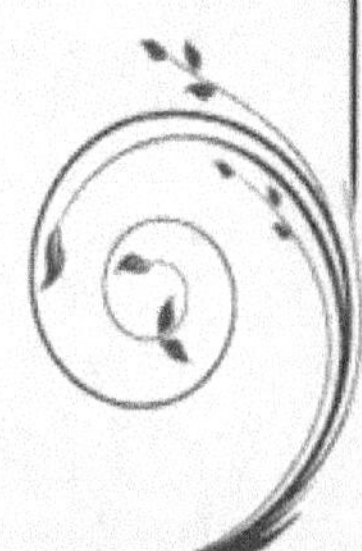

Good and bad.

EVERY GUSH OF BREATH

Is a lot and a lot more

It reminded those evenings

At the seaside of my small town

My home town smelled of jasmine

Freshly ground coffee and spices

What are these trees with red canopies

Murmuring to me when I glance across

The windows, to shed those leaves

Of memories and strive into the very

now of existence, eyes blazing

In feverish fret stares at people

Walking their dogs, smoking their

Worries out as fumes making

Different patterns in the air

Viruses or antibodies

Who would win

It is a fair game.

For I never fear death

I have looked in its eyes so cold

I have seen it stole my world ruthless

I knew it skin deep and declared my choice

My time at its behest

Quarantine is contemplation

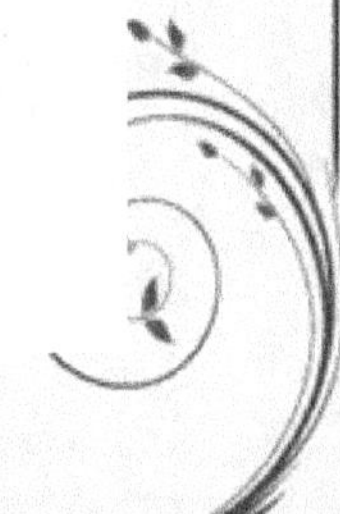

Of thoughts deeds and passions

Of all my life I felt I wrote it for love

Pain and Gains seems trivial

Passion just made me smile

I fancied the people who would think

The Drama queen is down.

Felt the old souls nearby who kindled

Lots of care and Just quoted these lines

It is this small life; we make a lot of fuss about it

The best part of it is...

The celebration of being alive and

For being there for whom we love and abide

MY WORDS FIND THEIR FREEDOM

In the vastness of your sky

Breaking every shackle of

Conforming notions it gives birth

to me a million times from the

decaying of yesteryear in to

sprouts of astounding tomorrow

I find my sustenance in the lucidity

of these moments which like ether

Is subtle and deep and deeper in the core.

Incessant drizzling rendering nothing

But the vacuum of this quantum reality

I look through the windows of your soul

In to the ocean deep oysters filled with

Eternal truths every being holds in and

To the green unbounded pastures

Of dreams with countless Hope's in it

I and you, the plurals

The alpha and Omega, the beginning and end.

The duality

The entangled mesh of matter.

Which blends as several notes

Reverberating along a path unknown

Where there is no more ignorance

In that infinite consciousness where

Love is a pure flow of serenity

Let me be the little joy of

glow worms that surprise your winter nights.

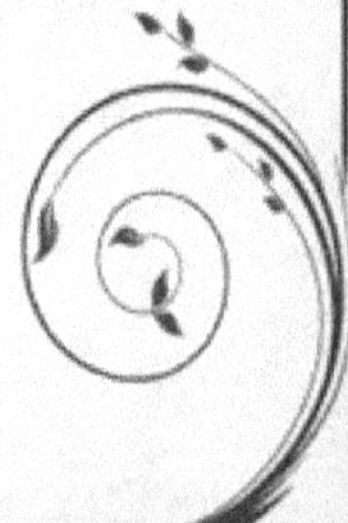

IF EVER THE EARTH COULD SAY

It is all about just love and

If ever could sky know it is

Deep within the core that

Never did alter in times.

With a thousand arms of rains and

Storms it could hold on in an embrace

For days and weeks until

Pain gives way to passion

Passion to faith and faith to trust.

If ever the sea could say

It is all about just love and

If ever could the moon know it is

True the sea just swelled with its

Highs and low tides and danced

For just a glance of a ray of little

Moonlight to fill the depth for time immemorial and still

goes on and on.

If ever a dewdrop could say

If ever the sun could know it in heart

If ever did a night lily sigh or a jasmine

Take pride in its fragrance.

A breeze knew of it and claimed its possessions...

If ever...

MY FIRST VERSES

When I scribbled my first verses

It rained a bit, drizzles like a maiden's ardent tears sky

bled unto my forehead with love

That man can never comprehend

Mom's pyre did burn down to ashes

Before my numb eyes that stared in to

Infinity holding my dad's trembling arms

Whispering hold on am there

I know not many a three year would

Mean it, but I meant it like a seedling

In a storm, lost but steadfast as ever

Until this very moment

Lost but not quite shattered withered

I still write for verses are my gift

Of fate, that time and tide could never

Take away from me in deceit nor else

Like the divine just embraced me

In his tight hold with words and with

Words he built a world for me

He won me friends that are special

Who loved just loves on sake

And never just hurt with hate and smitten

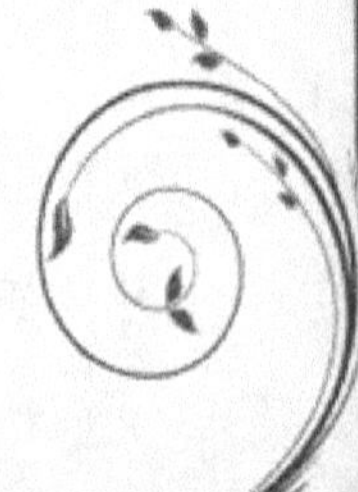

Envy nor let loose blasphemy and endless

Gossips on me that would one day cost them

What they cost for they know not what

They did, the pain inflicted and shame they spread with

tongues so loose.

The way they peeped into my wounds

And laughed at my scars never leaving them to

heal....but verses kept me live

I scribbled a lot.

I walk with a story untold in my heart

There is nothing like that the clouds of

Monsoon at its behest.

I still do scribble

Right and wrong

Between Right and wrong

Life for me has the same distance as time and rail

wheels.

It rolled on and on

Beyond the eyes of prejudices my verses

remain as love just true love.

unconditional and unimaginable...

The universe reverberated with it rhymed with it

unequivocally.

I still scribble....as that rainy day...

A FRIEND WITHIN

When you look into the self

Into deep within your soul

There you find a friend waiting

You never knew existed before

Someone so true and pious

Beaming with love and light

Who never made fuss or mess

But kept patiently waiting on

Until you tasted loneliness and

Willingly took the pain of dispelling

Myths around you ripping off the

Darkness and gazing the light

That enlightens your path ahead

You stand out as the serene

Pristine sparkling truth

Not identifying with the deeds

Not letting the past to breed as

The future but to burn in to

A present that is transcending and calm

You find your quest answered

In the fire of your knowing

In the abode of your master

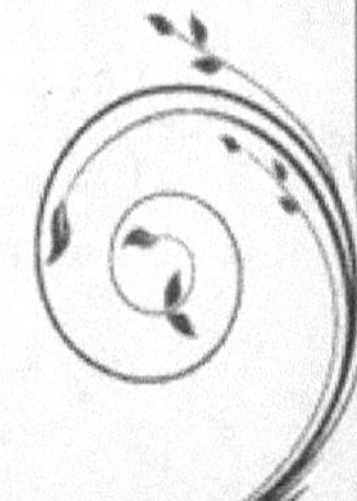

You are just a single petal

Of thought to which universe is

Reverberating and is in ultimate coherence

You realized you exist between the pauses

Of the two breaths and nothing but it

There is no grief no doubt no longing

But a stillness that walks in every walk

Of your life.

What would or could you call it

That friend from within

Who resides in this garment of our lifetime

This shrine of ours...

A divine friend that just waits.

ILLUSIONIST

Walk into the dias

Sparkling in your black and purple

Enchant the mob with your sapphire green

Prisms that pierce the soul and erase the time

Take me by your arm

The shackles of silence are burning in my heart

Rip down my veils and see through my scars

The promise is kept and forever buried deep in me it

flows through my veins my nerves

And makes me the tree the sap and nectar

Illusionist

Walk into the dias

Changing the rules and changing the nature

Making a new song that the world could dance along

with your love in your right arm

Trust in your left, faith in your right eye

Justice in the left, Righteous your smile

Let me just unleash myself in you

Until it just makes a finite from infinity

Illusionist

Walk into the dias

Let out a butterfly with glowing wings at night

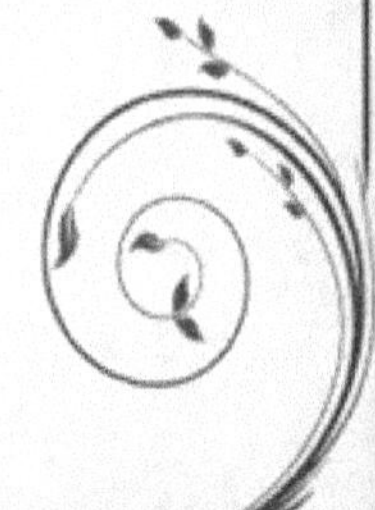

Let out three doves into eternity for the truth's sake and

bring forth a lamb, to caution the world

And with the tears of deep remorse

Let down a river on the very bank would

another yet another civilization could recite their

primordial hymn and thus

Let again a cycle to end begin and begin and end.

Illusionist

Walk into the dias

Let me just look into those eyes...

To begin and end.

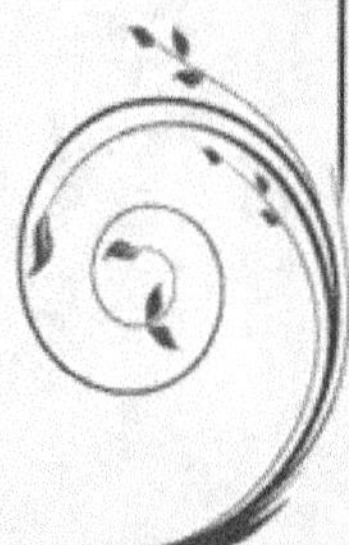

NOVEMBER

Another November

Yet another fall

Just withering away in to

Days that are shorter and

Nights longer...

Beneath the masked faces

People learned to converse

The new art of comprehension of each other

Despite a cell wall, a virus

Proved its might in skills of existence

Darwinian schools of thoughts

or esoteric primordial truth

Halloween costumes and sales lingered

Installs of very many malls

Taxicab driver murmured

Not looking up to Thanksgiving

Not this time...

Another cab driver just told her

Story of the little cozy house

The man she met at the crossroads

And the dreams she has for times ahead

Made the sunset look gleam

Yet subtle and ardent

Optician assured it is the age...

It is getting blurred my words these days

Still, she complimented

What wonderful large eyes

Beautiful indeed

Like a never adored altar

I looked into them...tears have dried up

I need to instill them in artificial.

Autumn that stole the light

Wrote darkness in the pages of fate

November comes and goes

Every leaves shed and revived

From death to life

It is a hell of a battle

It had a price to pay

But the heart has only one way to beat

One rhythm one love one prayer

Another November

A cold desk red sky and orange

Lush everywhere.

In this amber mind is not

restless any more

It is thoughtless merged

With stillness and beyond

IN THE DARK, IN THE DOOM

In the despondency

In the storm

Through and through

I will be there

Take my hand hold it tight

Oh my friend just trust

It right, though the sky

Is so black it would rain

And this too would

Pass and like a sun

You would emerge

True at the soul, pure in will

Strong is still the wounded

Lion and know it in heart

Guarded are your ways

Hold on to the Faith so deep

In the fire as hell

In the waters deep

In the space so lone

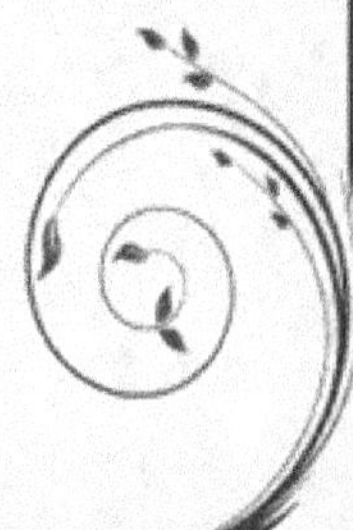

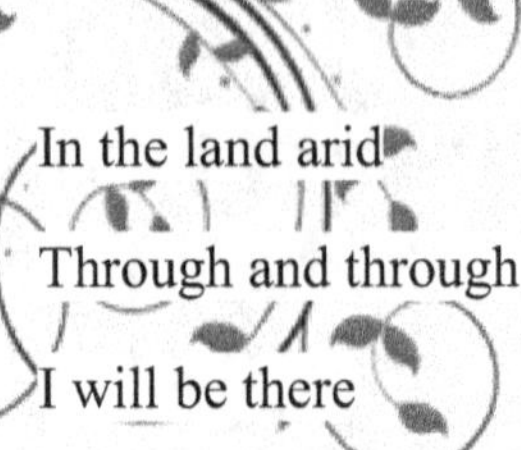

In the land arid

Through and through

I will be there

Like a single star that is left alone in the sky

When you are too tired and lost

To brighten up hope, I'll be there

Like a breeze so cool with its healing touch inherent, to calm you down and care

I'll be there.

Like a divine covenant that stays beyond

human perspectives to comprehend

I'll be there ....in need and deed

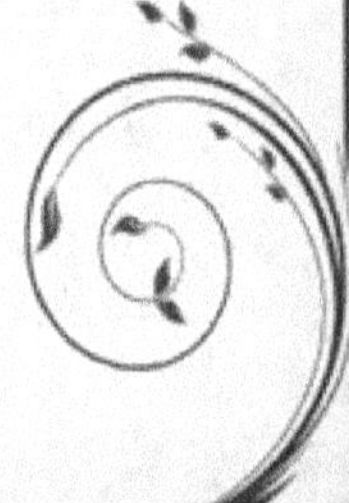

IN THE REBEL

In the antagonist, in the nonconformist in the deviant

In the dissenter in the outcast and outspoken

Incorrigible irreverent defamation of a century's
timeline,

A shadow conceals the stock character!

A mask a perfect smile deceives many tears!

The protagonist who lost the cause

is incarcerated and slew forever in the depth of
existential conflict to master the

the art of survival among the so-called fittest.

Succumbing the self at the feet of opinions of a
merciless mob of today's

That lost comprehension of anything like kindness,
ungrateful

The first person and second person

No more exists in the play

The omniscient decides the storyline

Voyers look into others life through

New windows of social media

Gossipers find orgies after orgies

By enjoying the pain of others

Treating their impotent souls

It takes courage to live a life shattered by a system and some people

No amount of apologies would

Heal the wounds that were made

Lives withered and crumbled in to

The deep darkness of internal rifts

Neurochemicals that got jarred in trauma

of nightmares of hellfire that one could

Ever pass through in a lifetime.

In the lost, but hoping

In the stumbling

Yet walking

In the forsaken but not lonely

In the broken but beautiful

There is a lot to see through

Instead of pointing fingers

You never know their journey

their story,

It takes very less time

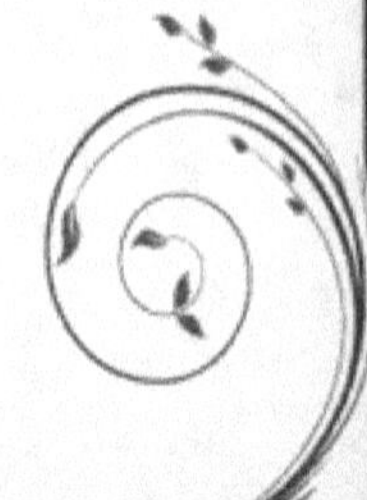

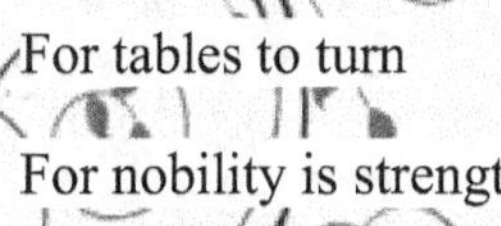

For tables to turn

For nobility is strength

It raises some

Love is another

Some are bound and fall ...just in it

Like fireflies.

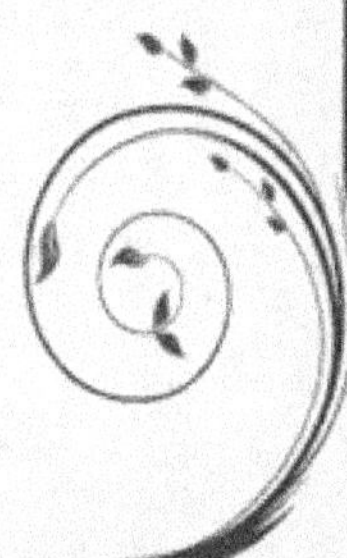

ABOUT THE AUTHOR

Anju Prasad , the author of the international books ,Love Anthems and Virginia Blues is an Msn RN who lives in United States of America .She has written many other poems and Novel in her native language and is a Reiki healer .Her initial works were more related to love and she had a stunning style of depicting nature and other symbols to integrate its colors .She never left the chance to use her narrative in questioning every conventions and belief systems which she felt were afflicting the minority .She considered herself as the voice of the unheard and her later works serves as bridge between existential and spiritual spheres .She takes her readers too with her quests and conquers , of pains and brokenness and tries find answers to some eternal questions along such poetic ventures .She is from a village of India and her poems are esoteric and exotic most often, while they find expansion in western skies, reminding the soulful expression and effort of Methodist writer.

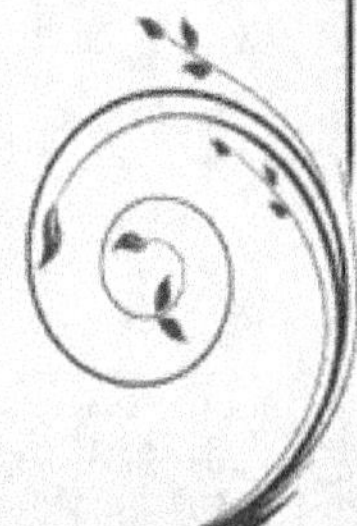